Peter Lancett is an author, editor and film maker with several published novels to his credit, including Seeing Red and Gun Dog, for Ransom Publishing. Recently he wrote and directed a feature film, The Xlitherman. Currently developing material for film and television, he divides his time between New Zealand and California.

IN THE SAME SERIES

Hanging in the Mist

PETER LANCETT

Ransom

Hanging in the Mist

PETER LANCETT

Series Editor: Peter Lancett

Published by Ransom Publishing Ltd.
Radley House, 8 St. Cross Road, Winchester, Hampshire, SO23 9HX, UK
www.ransom.co.uk

ISBN 978 184167 8795

First published in 2011
Copyright © 2011 Ransom Publishing Ltd.
Front cover photograph: Slobo Mitic

For my darling wife Alexandra,
the sine qua non of my life,

and for my Cara Soror,
Luxcandida...

Lux et Gemina Lumina

Love is all. Love under will.

CHAPTER 1

Well I think that this is working out pretty good. This recorder, I mean. It's dead light so it's no big deal to hold it, and when I tried it out earlier, the sound was dead good as well. And it records for hours on one of them little 'flash' cards. And it was dead easy to nick from that market stall. I've had loads of stuff from there. Mostly batteries and little stuff like that. But when I saw this thing, I just had to have it. It's dead trick. There was about six of em on the stall and it was a busy afternoon, so it was easy just to stuff one in me jacket when the bloke wasn't looking. A bit harder than slipping a packet of batteries up your sleeve, but no big deal. I wasn't scared or anything.

Market stalls are better to nick from than the shops. They have cameras and all that in the shops. And the big ones have store detectives and stuff. I've never been caught. But I know people who have. I stay away from the big shops. The guy that runs this stall is a dick anyway. He's a big bloke and he's big headed with it. I hear him when he's talking to people who're asking about the stuff he's selling; the cheap cameras and watches, and radios and DVD players and that. He's talking out of his arse and he doesn't know any better than the people who are asking.

Anyway, screw him. I'm back in me bedroom now, and it's funny standing on this wobbly computer chair in here. It's funny cos you'd think I'd be up high enough already, wouldn't you? Our flat being on the tenth floor of the block and everything. I hope this recorder thing is getting all this.

I can see out of the bedroom window from here. It's another shit day and it's dead cloudy and it was cold outside when I was down at the market. I can see chip papers blowing around and all the crap that people can't be arsed to put in the bins. I can even see one of the big bins in front of the shops and the chippie. It's been dented and bashed, and even though it's fixed into the ground, it's almost leaning over. Somebody's had a right go at kicking it out of the ground altogether. I know this for a fact, because I was one of the ones doing it. We'd already ripped one out over the other side of the estate and it was a bloody good laugh doing it. But this one just wouldn't budge. It's been a few months now, and nobody's come to fix it up or anything. Me mate Johnno has said we should finish it off properly sometime. But that would just be boring. Everything's boring around here.

I can see Marina Surtees now, crossing the big grass area in the middle of the estate. She's sticking to the path, even though it will take her the long way round. It makes sense cos I can see from how she's taking these dead little teetering steps that she's got her usual high heels on. It's late in the afternoon, but it's still daytime, and it's windy and cold and everything, but she's got this denim mini skirt on and a black tee shirt. I can't see from here but I bet it's got *Metallica* or something like that on it. She's well into metal and that, and her hair is dyed black all the time. Although sometimes you can see the roots showing through where it's growing out. Like me mum's.

One thing I can see from up here is Marina's tits. She's got big tits has Marina and she always has had. Well, for a long time anyway. She was an early starter. First to grow tits, first to go on the rag. All the other girls in school were always dead jealous of her back then. I'm buggered if I can see why. It's a bloody messy and smelly thing to have to go through every month if you ask me. If I was a girl, I would be praying for it not to happen. But I suppose for them, it's like a sign that they've grown up and everything. And I suppose us boys were no different really. I can remember all of us in the changing rooms at school inspecting the skin around Eddie Bassett's dick to see the first pubes that any of us had grown. We'd have been about ten or eleven then. And it wasn't long after that when the word went around that Eddie Bassett had fetched spunk. I can remember Johnno when he told me with a voice full of wonder. "He's more mature than us," Johnno had said at the time. I don't know why I remember those words, but I do, and the way he said them, and the look on his face. Funny what crap sticks in your mind, eh? Anyway, after that you can imagine loads of us boys wanking away every spare minute in an effort to be as 'mature' as Eddie Bassett. Sometimes we'd be doing it in a group, all of us inspecting each other like scientists looking for signs of jism. What a fucking laugh.

Mind you, I bet none of us have stopped doing it, even though all of us have been fetching spunk for years now. The evidence is all around for anyone to see. Four of the girls who were in the same class as me and Marina Surtees are already pushing prams and we're all only fifteen and sixteen. One girl, Kylie Erickson has two kids. They don't come to school much, the girls with babies, and you see them hanging out around the estate, smoking and talking to each other, babies either asleep in their pushchairs or screaming fit to bust. And the girls seem pretty natural as mums, like it's what they'd always wanted to be, and that all they were waiting for was to be sixteen so they'd get a council flat of their own and even more benefit money. One of the girls I know who has a baby was dead clever and all. She was right brainy, but here she is, a mum at fifteen and she acts and talks like this is all she ever wants to be. All she ever wanted to be. And maybe that's true, even though it seems stupid to me. She will at least get a council flat and her rent paid for and everything, and then she can live off benefits, and if she wants more money or a bigger place all she'll have to do is have more kids. It's more of a future than I'll ever have though.

And anyway, it's none of me business. I've thought about being lots of things, but what I wanted more than anything is to be a mechanic. I love cars and engines and that, and I love fixing things. I don't mind the oil and stuff. I just like cars and motors. I can see a car over there, all burned out and rusted. Somebody must have took it and then burned it out when they'd had their fun with it. You can hear cars at night, screaming round the estate. A little kid was killed by one last year. They never caught the kids who were driving the car, neither. I know who they are. I think a lot of people do. But you just don't talk when you live around here. Especially to the filth.

All the same, looking at that wrecked and burned out car, I can't help wanting to get a set of tools and go about fixing it up. It would take a long time but I could do it. Except for one thing. I haven't got any tools any more. Fucking bastards have pawned them. I bloody hate them, me so-called mum and dad. Bastard one and bastard two is more like it. It's not the first time they've taken stuff of mine and pawned it. Fucking pair of crack heads.

Funny thing is, despite what I said, I don't really hate em. I don't much like em though. But they're me mum and dad, and I live with them. We're not so unusual. Well actually, maybe we are. There aren't that many two parent families on this estate! Ha ha! Still, I'm used to them doing shit like this. All me life I've been promised stuff, had stuff to look forward to, but it's always turned out shit or never happened at all. There's always been some excuse.

There's a teacher at school who tries to encourage us to work. He's not such a bad bloke, I suppose, even though he is a bit of a div wearing market stall clothes and them crappy Jesus sandals all the time, but he wants us to do the best we can. He keeps saying that we should make the most of every opportunity because you only get one bite of the cherry. That's what he actually says: one bite of the cherry. Well I know what he means. And there have been loads of times when the cherry has been close to me mouth, but I've never had that bite. Bastard one or bastard two or both of em have always made sure it got knocked away.

Marina Surtees is just disappearing from sight now, round the back of the little council office with the wire over the windows. It's a shame. I liked watching her tits jiggle as she walked. Makes me think of the times I've seen em for real. Not that I've ever got off with Marina, or anything. But I did used to go out with her best mate, Sharlene Stokes, when Marina was going out with this biker bloke who was twenty. We used to go round his place a lot and all we ever did was watch telly and smoke and fuck. Sharlene's tits were nothing like Marina's. They were dead small actually. But I liked them. I liked Sharlene, come to that. But that didn't end well. Just another thing taken away from me.

Woah, shit! Nearly fell off the fucking chair. Cheap piece of crap. Wobbles all over the place.

It's getting darker outside now. Not properly dark yet, but I can see lights are on in a lot of the flats in the other tower blocks. And the street lights have just come on down below. There's only a little lamp on here in me bedroom and if I try, I can see me reflection back from the window. It's not a pretty sight. Both eyes black, bottom lip all swollen up on the left side and me cheeks are all swollen and bruised. It's shit being me.

CHAPTER 2

The last two weeks have been shit. And not just cos it's been cold and rainy most of the time. I don't suppose I'm ever going to be a mechanic. Me mum was supposed to have filled in this form and sent it to the school. Well, she didn't even have to fill it in cos I'd done that. All she had to do was sign it.

What it was, was that the school had arranged this week away at this place where you can have a practice at what it's like to be a mechanic or an electrician or a plumber or whatever. It's dead good and I know people who've been. Well part of it is, you have to get your mum or your dad to sign the form to say that it's all right for you to go, and that you have got the stuff that they want you to take with you. It's mostly clothes and overalls and that, but for the mechanic course, they need you to have a socket set and a screwdriver set and an adjustable wrench. I reckon they must have had that stuff there at one time but they've got so sick of having it nicked that they make you bring your own now. Anyway, I have me own socket set, one that I got from a car boot sale. It's only a cheap one, but all the bits are there and I've used it when I've helped fix up the cars of some of the petrol heads on the estate. Not that they need my help, but some of em let me help them anyway, and I learn tons off them. Sometimes they even take me out for a burn in their cars and that is well cool. Kyle Watson has this dead trick Vauxhall Corsa. It's got these green LEDs under the sills that match the metal flake paint job, and an oversized air box and filter in the engine and stuff, and a stiffened suspension. I helped him fit that. It sounds amazing when he floors it. He's eighteen and he works at Halfords, the big car parts place on the retail park. He gets a discount, so his car always looks dead good.

Anyway, I gave bastard number two – me mum – this form to sign, over a month ago. The one thing I hadn't got was an adjustable wrench, but I said I'd save up and get one. I never nick anything from car or hardware shops; those are places that I like going to and I get advice from the blokes who work there and that, which is well cool of em. Bastard number one – that's me dad – chips in and says not to worry and that he'll sort me one out. Not that I believed a word of that though. They was both spaced out on skunk when I asked em, so all I was interested in was getting the form signed. Me mum said to leave it out for her and that she'd sign it later. Well that was OK, but I know better than to trust anything she says when she's spaced out, so I wrote a note reminding her, that she'd read when she was sensible again. Probably the next morning. But I wasn't worried, cos there was two weeks to get that form back to the school. Well next day the form wasn't on the table, so I figured me mum had taken it and signed it and that it was probably in her bag. Anyway, I asked her for it when I saw her, and she said that she'd taken it in to the school when she'd been passing earlier in the day. I believed her, cos she has done that once or twice before. And it's not like she has work or anything to consider, so she does have the time.

All the same, I should have checked, I should have checked. Old man Cooper, who takes us for metal work and who had organised this trip away, had been off sick. I could have gone to the office and checked though, but I couldn't be arsed. She promised me she'd taken the form in, and cos she had done before, I just believed her. Of course, she hadn't taken it in. Two weeks ago last Friday was the last day to get the forms in, and when we went for metal work, which was the last class of the day, Cooper asked me where me form was. I told him me mum had brought it to the school. Cooper gave me a bollocking in front of everybody, saying how I'd been lucky to have been chosen and that somebody else could have had me place. All the same, he went to check with the office and I had to stand there in class with everybody taking the piss out of me and that. And when he came back and said that nobody had brought the form in, and that it was too late now and I wouldn't be going, I could feel meself getting madder and madder. Me cheeks were going red, I could tell, but worse, me eyes were beginning to fill up. I couldn't let everybody see me cry, so I just pushed past everybody and ran out of that classroom, with Cooper shouting out after me. I wasn't listening, so the only word that I could remember was "detention". As if I cared.

Out of the school I ran, through the streets all the way home, and the freezing cold wind burned against me cheeks where the tears had run down, but I didn't care. I don't even know if I wanted her to be in when I got home. I can't remember if I wanted to shout at her or if I felt like I never wanted to see her worn out face ever again. She knew how much I wanted to be a mechanic. She knew how much going on this course meant to me. It wasn't like I'd asked her for money or anything. I'd paid to go on it out of me own pocket and everything. All she'd had to do was sign a poxy fucking form. And she couldn't even be arsed to do that. How could she do that to me, eh? Being a mechanic was all I'd dreamed about since I was little. She knew that. She fucking well knew.

And when I got in she was there, with bastard number one. I could hear em talking and whispering in their bedroom. I just burst right in cos I was past caring. They were sitting on the bed with nothing on, me mum with her sagging tits showing and everything, and him with it all hanging out and neither of them with a care in the world.

"Hey babe," she drawls, "how yer been? Come on in and sit down a minute."

I saw it in her eyes before I ever noticed the gear on the bed between them. Cranked up, both of em were. Then I could smell it, and I could see the glass pipe in his hand. I know there's rocks of filthy crap in that glass bowl, and he's holding a light under

it so that the rocks inside start to sp
and crackle, and then he's sucking on it,
sucking all the smoke in, but I don't care
about him. It's her, the bitch.

"How could you do that to me?" I
screamed, but her glazed eyes told me she
didn't know what the fuck I was on about.
So I scream it at her again.

She starts to get up off the bed like
she's in slow motion and I can see the
white stretch marks on her sagging tits,
and everything else as she unfolds her legs
from under her with no shame whatsoever.
I'm ashamed and embarrassed though,
even while I'm angry, even though I've seen
them like this more often than I'd like, and
I can't look at her other than to stare into
those blank black eyes. Come to think of
it, seeing this sight once would have been
more often than I'd have liked. And it's
been loads more than once.

She hasn't answered me, so I scream at
her again. "How could you do that to me?"

"Do what babe?" she asks, all innocent, holding her arms out towards me. "What's the matter? What's happened? Come and sit here and tell me, eh?"

I hate that slurring voice she has when she's spaced, and I just pushed her away, so that she fell back on the bed, giggling. She turns to him, like he's even noticing that either of us are there at this point. "Oooh," she drawls, "Was it something I done then, babe?"

Right then I could have killed her. I was biting me bottom lip and I know that me fists were clenched tight. "It's what yer didn't do, yer fucking crack whore!"

"Ay, watch how yer talk to yer mother."

I just turned on him when he said that. "Or what'll yer do?" I screamed "C'mon, yer whacked out bastard, what'll yer do?"

"Chill out man," was all he could reply and I'd heard him say that so many times that I still can't understand why I didn't just give him a few good slaps right then. But it was her I was more interested in.

"You knew how much it meant to me. You knew! It's all I've ever wanted to do and all you had to do was sign the fucking form! Why did you lie to me? Why?"

I'm screaming, but she just sits there with her arms wide open so I can see old track lines on the insides of em, and her mouth is open and she's shaking her head like she really doesn't understand what I'm on about. Which is probably about right.

I spotted that big suede hippy bag of hers on the floor by the bed, so I lunged down and grabbed it, tipped it up so that everything fell out all over the place. Old hankies, half empty boxes of Tampax, pens, a purse, and loads more dirty crap that it's not worth listing. But one thing stood out to me. The form I'd given her. The form she'd told me she'd handed in to school. I snatched it up from among a load of used tissues, and I waved it till me arm was fit to drop off. "You said you'd handed this in at school for me. And now it's too late, and I can't go on the course! Why did you tell me you'd handed it in?"

She just shrugged again and shook her head. "Sorry babes," she slurred. "I must have forgot."

"These things happen lad," bastard number one chipped in at this point. "Yer should have reminded us."

Something about that stopped the screams in me throat. Yeah, bastard number one was right. I should never have had faith in either of em. Never. I looked down at that form right then. She hadn't even signed it.

"You didn't even fucking sign it," I said.

"Oh," she said. "Do I have to sign it? Gimme a pen . . ."

She's too far gone to even shout at.

"I'll never get a chance like this again. I'd paid for it as well. You know how much I hate doing cleaning down at that place."

"Hey, that's a good job, that," bastard number one chips in. "Nice perks. See if you can get some steak again on Saturday. They won't notice a few steaks out of all that lot."

Like he's ever done a day's work anywhere. Much less worked at some disgusting stinking place like the abattoir. I just looked down at him saying that, and the anger just drained out of me. All I felt right then was pity. And I could feel right away that it was wrong. You shouldn't have to feel pity for your mum and dad like that. But they disgusted me. And I realised that they had for a long time.

"You bastards have never done anything for me," I said all calm, like. "All I asked you to do was sign a form. I've got the money to buy the wrench I needed – I bloody knew better than to believe you when you said that you'd get me one. And all the other tools I've already got."

A look on his face stops me even though I've got tons more to say.

"What have you done?" I ask. He just looks down at the filthy little bag on the bed between them and right then I know. I just know.

"We had to babes," she cries out, all plaintive. "We was desperate."

I didn't say anything, but I turned and shot out of that room. And when I burst into me own room, the one I'm in now, I didn't even have to look. But I did look. I slid to the floor and lifted that loose hanging duvet and there was nothing under the bed. The red metal toolbox was gone. Did I cry? Well I don't suppose it matters much if you know now, so yeah, I cried. I sobbed for a few seconds, and could have killed meself for not putting the toolbox away in the locked cupboard where I keep most of me stuff. I'd just been lazy, and now it was all gone. Everything. Gone.

I rushed back into their room and they were swapping that fizzling glass pipe between them like I'd never even been there at all. I swiped it out of their hands and it smashed against the walls.

"Hey," bastard number one called out, but I turned on him and even through me tears he must have seen the anger in me, cos he just backed away.

"Oh don't be like that, babes. We'll make it up to you . . ." She said more but I didn't listen, just tipped over her bedside table and smashed the lamp standing on it. It was all I could think to do. I was supposed to be helping Kyle with his car next day. Now I wouldn't even be able to do that. Christ, the bastards.

Yeah, that was a great Friday, two weeks ago. And me hand is tight and sweaty gripping this recorder as I remember it. I'd better not squeeze too hard. It's only plastic and I don't want to break it. Ha ha.

I'm still standing on me wobbly computer chair, but me balance is better now. I'm looking down to that space under me bed though. It's still empty. And that's how I feel inside.

CHAPTER 3

It's funny, the way that even though I'm standing on this chair, the frame of the bunk bed is still higher than me. I can put me hand on the frame and lean against it a bit. I still can't believe it, the way they got us the bunk bed. We never got presents or anything, hardly even at Christmas or on our birthdays. So it was amazing when they got us this. We really needed it as well. And even though we had to put it together ourselves – well it was me who did it, mostly – it was still a brilliant surprise. I still don't know where it come from or how much it cost, or even if they paid for it at all. But I didn't care then and I still don't.

Hanging in the Mist

There used to be two grotty beds stuffed into this room with not much space left for anything else. Me and me sister used to share this room right up until she left and got a flat of her own. She got one off the council, just after the baby came, one in that tower block I can see way across the estate. I was glad as hell as well, cos I'd had to sleep on the settee after she had the baby. I couldn't share the room no more.

I can't see her actual flat from here, even though I can see the block it's in, cos it's on the other side, overlooking the dual carriageway. I've been over there and you can't hear the traffic. But you can sit and watch it. You wouldn't hear the traffic anyway, cos her baby is screaming all the time. It never shuts up. I've sat and held it and sometimes for a minute it will lie back and gurgle and smile. But it's never long before it's screaming and puking. Or it's done something worse. Me sister says she's dead happy having a place of her own. She's only seventeen but she doesn't look like she did before the baby came. She's still a lot heavier and she looks dead tired all the time. And most of the time she's just slopping around in grey track pants and baggy tee shirts and that, and slippers. Still, she gets help from Social Services and that. They come around twice a week. Still a lot for a seventeen year old girl to have to deal with though. I couldn't do it. And she's all on her own and that. There's no father of the baby around helping her or giving her money. She says she doesn't even know who the father is. When she told me that, I didn't ask anything else. I didn't want to think about what she might have been up to.

One thing is for sure, it was getting cramped sharing our bedroom until the council gave her that flat. We'd been sharing it all of our lives. I used to get embarrassed, getting dressed and undressed. I'd wait until she was out of the room or something, or if I went to bed after her, I'd make sure all the lights were out before I got undressed, or if she had her reading light on when she was going through old celeb magazines and that, I'd get in bed and get undressed under the covers. She never cared though.

She would just strip off and get changed as often as she liked and she never seemed embarrassed. She probably got that off our cracked-up mum and dad.

I'd never tell her this, but I have to say I'm not surprised that she ended up getting knocked up. Counting back, it must have been when she went on that holiday to Spain last year. From what her and her mates were saying when they got back, it sounds like they was on the piss all the time from the moment they got there. And they'd been shagging everything that moved and took the slightest interest. Anyway, that's how the holiday sounds, the way they tell it. So like I say, no wonder . . .

I like looking out of the window at this time of day. It's dark, but it's not quite night. I can see the street lights on below, and I can see car headlights and stuff, and I can still make out people on the green between the blocks of flats and in front of the shops and that. And in the tower blocks, some of the flats have lights on and some are still dark. You can see this blue flicker from some of the others where there is a telly playing but no lights on.

It's kind of eerie staring out of the window at this time of day, especially at this time of year when it's got dark dead early and it's cold outside. I mean, you can't hear anything from up here and through the double glazing anyway, but you just know that it's sort of quiet down there. Maybe if there's wind blowing, you'd hear that down there, but it's quiet in a way that it never is in the summer, like. In the summer, people are not in any kind of hurry to get where they're going. They're probably just outside for the hell of it, cos it's warm and everything. And kids are out playing late as well. But at this time of year, everybody seems wrapped up in heavy clothes and if they're out at all, they're always hurrying to be someplace. Someplace warm. And I think it's that, the way that everyone wants to be somewhere and not caring about the outdoors at all, is what makes it feel quiet. I know, I know, Old Duckworth, the nerd-geek who teaches science at school, would probably say it's all in me head, that, or give me some kind of bloody stupid explanation that would be dead boring or something. But I don't care. I think it seems quieter now because of what I just said. And Duckworth isn't here. So fuck him.

There's Kyle's green Vauxhall Corsa, just pulling into the estate. I can see the green glow from underneath from the LEDs. I'll never have a car like that. And now Kyle's stopping outside the shops and getting out. He's probably going to get some chips or something for his tea. I've seen him go to the chippie loads of times from up here. Yep, there he goes, into the chippie. It'd be great to just jump in his car now, while he isn't looking, and take it for a burn down the dual carriageway. What a blast that would be. And get it back before he came out of the chippie so he never knew it had even gone. But there's loads of reasons that could never happen. Kyle would kill me if he ever found out. And he'd know right away when his car started, with that big air filter and that phat exhaust giving it that deep growl. And you'd never even get it started anyway, cos there's an immobiliser that he had fitted by the blokes who do that where he works. These are just daydreams, little stories I make up in me head when I'm looking out of the window. It's dead boring living here, so you have to. And anyway, I'd never do anything like that to Kyle, even if I could and even if I thought I could get away with it. I still think he's solid, even after everything that's happened. Which I will be talking about, only later on.

I've already said how me crack whore mother had fucked up me chance to go on this mechanics course. Well, that afternoon after I'd smashed up their bedroom a bit and left them strung out and shouting at me to come back and how they'd make it up to me and everything, I just stormed out of the flat, slamming all the doors, probably hoping that I'd break something if I'm honest.

I stopped crying when I was in the lift going down. And I wiped the tears away. I didn't have much idea what I wanted to do, but I found meself at the bus stop, and when the next bus came I got on it and went to the town centre. While I was on the bus, I kept asking meself how they could do that to me. I mean, selling me tools like that, me socket set, me screwdrivers, me spanners. I'd paid for all them meself, so they had no business touching them. And just for filthy crap to get zonked out with.

But then you know, that's just like them. It's the crap that comes first with them. It even comes before me and me sister and it always has. Weed, smack, blues, Es, coke, whatever – they had to be doing something. Even if that meant me and me sister going without. It's been like that our whole lives.

Actually, me very first ever memory, the farthest back that I can remember, is when I would have been five. I can't remember it all, what happened and that, but what I do remember is me and me sister standing outside on the landing outside our flat, with the wind blowing through a broken window at the end, and it's the middle of the night – so me sister tells me. And I'm crying and wailing and screaming and me sister is holding me hand and trying to get me to calm down and that. And our next door neighbour comes out to see what all the racket is about. Mrs Newton her name was and she was this big West Indian woman and her family was from Jamaica. Anyway, she came out asking what all the noise was about. And me sister said that me mum and dad were out and hadn't come home and that we were scared. Me sister has told me that this was something she made up. The truth was, the bastards were zonked out in their bedroom and they'd been on a three day bender, with people coming and going all the time, and they'd been skulking alone doing fuck knows what in their bedroom and just leaving us to fend for ourselves. Even at seven, me sister had had the brains to make up a story and not tell Mrs Newton the truth. She's definitely got the brains out of all of us.

I can remember Mrs Newton taking us in and she made us warm milk and she had these Jamaican ginger biscuits, which I still like and nick from the corner shop every now and then, and then she made me have a bath, cos apparently I was filthy. Like I say, mum and dad hadn't paid any attention to us whatsoever for over three days. Me sister was filthy as well, so Mrs Newton gave her a bath too. I don't remember much more of it, but I can remember lying on Mrs Newton's settee, wrapped up in a blanket, with me sister lying the opposite way, and Mrs Newton leaning over me and stroking me forehead and singing this Jamaican song with a dead soft voice.

I still sometimes think about Mrs Newton. She lived in that flat next to us right up until she died, about two years ago now. Her husband had left her ages before and her kids had all grown up and got married and got places of their own. So she died all alone. Her daughter found her when she came round to visit one Saturday. She let herself in with her key and found her mum sitting dead in her armchair with the telly still on. A heart attack it was, or at least that's what I heard. But whatever it was, it made me cry. She'd always been dead kind to me, and there had been loads of times when me and me sister had gone to sit in her flat and watched the telly with her when we were little and when bastard number one and bastard number two had gone out and left us on our own. I think I probably loved her.

Anyway, like I was saying, I went into the town, and I just walked around for a while. Even then, it was starting to get dark and I was cold and everything, cos I hadn't got a coat on. So I just went into the shops, not really looking at stuff or anything, just enjoying how clean it all was and how warm it was. And I think that cos there were just normal looking people in them it seemed to feel more comfortable. It didn't cheer me up exactly, but I wasn't feeling as upset as I had been. I was still dead angry though. And I kept thinking about smacking the pair of them up and kicking them and laying into them. It's amazing how many times you can play a scene like that in your head.

In one big department store I saw these dead soft big scarves and I thought how me sister would like one. I hung around there for a few minutes and I was thinking about whether I could nick one for her. But

I thought better of it. I've said before how the big stores have cameras and detectives and that. And really, I didn't feel up to it so it was like I would have been bound to get caught. So I went out again and it was nearly properly dark now.

Down the street was this big HMV shop where they sell DVDs and CDs and computer games and that. I always go in there and look. And I like it that they play music dead loud in there. It's not always stuff that I like, but I think that playing stuff dead loud like they do makes the place feel exciting and it gives you a lift. So anyway, that's where I went.

The place was pretty full and there were people and pushchairs in the aisles so you had to squeeze to get past sometimes. I started off, looking at the DVDs. I start at the beginning usually and go through all of them. I never get tired of that for some reason, even though I've done it hundreds of times. And it's funny how I seem to pick out the same covers all the time, and read the back of them like I've never seen them before. Old films like Terminator 2 which I've seen loads of times as well, and Hellraiser and that. I love those kinds of films – sci-fi and horror. I like films like that with loads of effects and loads of action. And I like films where there's lots of good fighting and violence and that.

Down at the bottom end of the shop, when I got there, I saw some kids that I knew from school. They didn't live on the same estate as me, but they lived on the council estate not far from me, all of them. There was five of them, Dave Martins, Josh Roberts, Danny Harrigan, Carrie Edwards and Lindsay Crocker. No surprise, they were all dressed in black and they'd got loads of make up on and that, cos they're Goths. They were looking at CDs and I got talking to them, cos I know them pretty well, even though I'm not a Goth or anything meself. Josh Roberts is in me class at school. He'd been there that afternoon when I'd run out of the class. Obviously we had to talk about what had happened, and I told them about how bastard number two had fucked up me chance of going on the course.

"So you can't go on it at all?" Lindsay asked me. If she hadn't got that stupid black lipstick on and that big heavy black jacket with chains all over it, and black nail varnish, and them big heavy black boots that look like Frankenstein should be wearing them, I reckon she'd look alright. I might even fancy her.

Well I told them how it was too late now, and I couldn't go, and how the two bastards had sold me tools and stuff anyway, and they were pretty cool about it and said how it was dead shitty and that. And while it didn't make up for anything, I did feel a bit better talking to them. And for a while we stood at the back of HMV, looking at the covers of CDs – bands I'd never even heard of like 'My Dying Bride', and 'My Arms, Your Hearse' and weird stuff like that – and talking about the shitty things that had happened to us all.

Then Lindsay says to me, "We're going over to Letisha's place in a bit. You fancy coming?"

She looks at the others and Josh says "Yeah, you should come along. We're just going to hang out and play music. Do some smoke . . ."

He grins as he says that last bit. Thing is, because of living with bastard number one and bastard number two all me life, I've never been interested in doing any of that stuff. You know that I'm not a goody two-shoes or anything feeble like that, but I just see how they are half the time and I don't want to be anything like them. But I don't want to go home right now either. So I said "yeah, what the fuck . . ?" And off we went.

CHAPTER 4

Letisha Simpson is nineteen and she has a baby and lives over on the far side of my estate. She's got a flat in the block next to the one where me sister lives, actually. We'd got the bus back from town and by the time we got to the estate, it was properly dark, even though it wasn't late or anything. About six o'clock I'd say.

As soon as we got off the bus, Josh got a packet of fags out of his pocket. He passed them around and asked if I wanted one. Well I don't do blow and all that, but smoking fags is something that I sometimes do. I like it, but sometimes I think it's a waste of money, like. It's different if I can get some knocked-off ones for next to nothing. Sometimes you can, if kids have knocked off a corner shop or that, and they'll sell you a pack for a quid. Other than that though, I'd rather spend me money on tools or computer games for me playstation and that. Mind you, after what the bastards did, I'd have been better off if I had blown everything on fags and booze I reckon. Cos what use are them tools to me now? I don't even know where they are.

Anyway, it was starting to get foggy and we're all sitting on this sort of concrete bench next to the grass square in the middle of all the tower blocks, and we've all got one of these fags that Josh has handed around. I held mine up to me nose. It smelled dead funny, but it was a proper fag, not a hand rolled spliff. Josh saw me sniffing at it and he laughed, but it was not like he was laughing at me or anything. At least it didn't feel like that.

"Don't stress, mate," Josh said. "These are clove cigarettes. That's where the scent comes from. This ain't no wacky-baccy."

I must have looked a bit stupid, and Lindsay says, "Don't you smoke blow then?" and when I shook me head, she says, "What, never?"

Well, I told her about bastard number one and bastard number two and said that I never wanted to be like them. And Lindsay says, "So it's like you're rebelling by not doing smoke or anything."

I hadn't ever thought of it like that before, but I have to admit there might be something in that. I'd been doing exactly what they wouldn't understand. And it made me laugh to think of it.

Dave started in then. "So if you started wearing a home made cardigan you'd really be sticking it to them, right?"

Carrie says, "And you could get some of them slippers, you know, like tartan bootees that zip up the middle."

"And one of them beige anoraks," Danny said, and he was already laughing.

And before you knew it, we was making up stupider and stupider things, and we were all laughing like it was the funniest thing any of us had ever heard. And thinking about it now, it's like I'm watching us all from high up here, looking down at us sitting on that concrete bench, through the fog and the orange streetlights and with the headlights from the odd car that turned into the estate. And we're all smoking these clove cigarettes, and I'm coughing me lungs up at first cos they're dead dry and dead strong, and the others are laughing even more. And it's like although I'm here, far away and up in the bedroom of our flat, and it happened two weeks ago, I can smell that strange sweet scent from them fags. And I can see the smoke, caught up in the air around us and it's making patterns, like how clouds make patterns. And the smoke seems to take ages to drift away in the orange light, like it's just hanging there in the mist. I've never been happier than I was in those moments, in all of me life.

Well, we smoked them fags and even if there was nothing wacky about that baccy, it's a strange fact that we were all loose and giggling as we walked on over to Letisha's tower block. I didn't even feel cold anymore cos everything was dead funny. And when we got to the bottom of the tower block, we pushed the main door open and went in.

The hallway was covered in tags and stuff, the same tags that keep appearing and then getting scrubbed off and then reappearing all over the estate. It didn't bother me though. A tag's a tag. They're everywhere. And anyone can get a spray can of paint.

Dave stood by the lifts pressing the buttons. None of the lights came on. But Dave kept on pressing anyway. The rest of us just hung about, not saying much of anything, waiting for the lift.

Two little kids came in and kicked open the door with a bang that startled us. They must have been about ten I reckon. I didn't recognize them. They stood staring at us for a few seconds, grinning and looking at each other. One of them turned towards Carrie.

"Are you Dracula's sister?" this kid asked.

Carrie just rolled her eyes, saying "Fuck off!" to the ceiling.

The kids looked at each other and laughed. It was such a silly thing that you couldn't take offence. They were just being kids.

Then the other kid points at Lindsay's boots. "Did you nick them off Frankenstein?" he asks. Now both of them are almost doubled up in that doorway, laughing. I was grinning too. I couldn't help it.

"You should be scared," Danny says to the kids. "The sun has gone down and us vampires need to taste blood." He's stretching out his arms and pretending to appear threatening. It's all good natured stuff. Obviously they get a lot of this from kids, dressing the way they do, and what Danny is doing is the best way of making sure that nothing gets out of hand. Like he told me later, you need a sense of humour to dress like that in the first place. Which

I thought was strange, since they seem to go out of their way to appear miserable all the time. I was beginning to see that that was just an act though. They'd done a lot of laughing since I'd been with them.

The kids just stood and watched as Danny started to climb the stairs, Danny complaining that it was going to be a bloody long hike and swearing about the lifts not working. The stairs were concrete, just like in our block and the walls were bare concrete too, covered with the tags we'd seen in the hallway downstairs, and our footsteps echoed. Eight flights up it was, to the landing where Letisha's flat was. And while we were joking about and laughing at the start, by the time we got there, we were all quiet and breathing hard. Carrie looked like she was going to be sick.

When we got to Letisha's door, Josh knocked on it. He had to knock hard cos you could hear this music coming from inside the flat. When the door opened, this girl was standing there. I'd seen her around the estate a few times but I didn't know her to speak to. Anyway, she was dressed in Goth gear as well, all moody black and with that black lipstick and nail polish like it was part of a uniform for them all. Obviously I stood out from the others but I didn't feel awkward or anything. Anyway, they all hugged and Josh introduced me, and Letisha gave me a hug as well, which felt kind of strange but at the same time kind of nice, and we all bundled inside.

Letisha turned the music down and Carrie went into the kitchen while the others slumped down onto bean bags and onto an old sofa that was a bit worn out but had once been covered with this purple fabric. There was a lot of purple in Letisha's flat. Even the walls were painted purple in the living room, and there were a few candles around the place and a joss stick burning so there was this thick sweet scent. I'd never been anywhere like it and while I thought it was dead weird, I thought it was dead cool as well. It was like it was warm and comfortable being dark like that.

Letisha sat cross legged on the floor and said, "Well, who's gonna crash the hash?"

I thought she was on about weed or something, but Danny reached inside a pocket and took out a pack of those clove fags we'd been smoking earlier. The pack was passed round and when it was offered to me, I remember I just shook me head.

Letisha said "What's up? Don't you like these? I've got some Silk Cut if you want an ordinary fag."

I told them that I hadn't got any of me own, so I shouldn't really be smoking theirs, but Danny just told me not to be stupid and that I should sit down and chill out and have a fag if I wanted one. So I took one from the pack and soon the smell of the clove fags was mixing with the smoke from the joss stick and in the candlelight it seemed like we were sitting in another world, not on our estate at all.

Carrie came back from the kitchen and she was carrying this tray with these glasses on it. The glasses didn't match or anything, but I could see that there was one for each of us, and she came round to all of us and we all took one. I couldn't tell what was in it and I was looking at it like it was something we'd made up in the chemistry lab at school, cos it was purple, like the walls and the bean bags and the cushions.

Lindsay said, "Don't worry, it isn't blood," and everybody laughed. Then she said, "Why don't you sit down and get loose? You look all itchy standing there like that." And so I sat down on the floor next to where she was lying across a big bean bag.

"What is this then?" I asked.

Josh raised his glass and said "Blood of the Prince!" and everyone raised their glasses as well, and said "Blood of the Prince" and skulled back their drinks in one. I was left holding mine and felt like a bit of a twat.

Lindsay nudged me, smiling, and said, "Go on, knock it back. It's only vodka and black currant."

So I raised me glass like they'd all done and said "Blood of the Prince" and knocked it back in one, and they all cheered.

"So you're not a Goth?" Letisha asked me. I just shook me head. "So what are you doing with this lot then?" she went on.

I told her that I just knew them from school and we'd met up in town and had been hanging out for a bit.

She looked at me for a second and then said, "Don't you normally hang out with them petrol heads off the estate?"

I said that I liked to help them work on their cars and that I was interested in cars and that, but that I didn't really hang out with them.

"Until your olds cashed in all your tools," Carrie said. "That was a shit trick."

Letisha looked puzzled, so I had to explain about how I had a crack whore for a mother and a bone idle bastard of a father.

I wasn't embarrassed saying it. Letisha just nodded like it was pretty common, and we sat around quietly for a minute smoking the clove fags and just chillin' to the music that was still playing. I knew the song even though I didn't know what it was called or who sang it. It had been at the beginning of a film I'd watched on the telly one time, called Donnie Darko. It was a dead weird film and I didn't really get what was happening in it, but it was pretty good at the same time and I liked it.

Danny said to Letisha, "Where's Bram?" and I must have looked puzzled cos Lindsay said, "Bram's Letisha's baby."

Letisha said that the baby was with her mother for the night and that she was picking him up in the morning. At least I knew it was a boy then, cos I'd never heard that name before. I asked, "What's Bram short for? I've never heard of that name."

Letisha said, "It's not short for anything. It's the name of a writer. Bram Stoker."

I had to say that I'd never heard of him. I don't read books much – except for car repair manuals and that. Books are dead boring. But I didn't tell them that.

"You've heard of Dracula, haven't you?" Carrie said. "Well he's the bloke who wrote it."

"You should read it some time," Letisha said. "Then you'd know what being a Goth is all about."

When she said that, it suddenly struck me that she was assuming that I wanted to become a Goth; but that was something I hadn't even thought about. Still, it did make me think about it for a minute right then. Cos it was dead cool just sitting there in Letisha's flat drinking vodka and black and smoking clove fags and listening to these songs that seemed to fit the candles and the dark and the way the others looked and dressed and that. And we was just having the mintest time. Yeah, I could dig it.

CHAPTER 5

And that was how it was for a couple of hours or so. We just sat around in the candlelight, listening to music and smoking and drinking vodka and black and laughing and fooling around. And I just loved it. Of course we were all getting drunk. And I noticed that Danny was getting closer and closer to Letisha until somehow they were on that sofa and they were "getting into romantic territory" as me sister puts it, and not minding the rest of us in the slightest. And we didn't mind them. At the time, it didn't even strike me as strange that Letisha was nineteen and that Danny was only sixteen. Thinking about it later I suppose it was a big difference. But we were all happy and having fun.

Then Lindsay said, "You know, you're dead pale and dead thin. You really would look good as a Goth."

I had to admit that I am dead pale, cos I don't much like being out in the sun, and I am pretty thin. But we was just messing about. And right then, Danny and Letisha got up off the sofa and headed off to Letisha's bedroom. Nobody said anything and the rest of us drank more vodka and Josh rolled a spliff. The others shared it with him, but I didn't have any, for all the reasons I've said before.

Anyway, we were all pretty drunk and Josh and Carrie and Lindsay and Dave were pretty stoned as well, and the talk got back to me being a Goth and that. I told them that I didn't think I could look like that and have everybody staring at me and everything, and anyway, I didn't think I'd like wearing all that black lace and stuff.

Lindsay said, "Honest, with your face and all that, you'd really look lush. You already look pretty wasted."

That was when Danny and Letisha came back. And they joined in saying I should try it.

Lindsay said, "Come on. Let me put some make up on you, see how you'd look."

And everyone was saying yeah, go on, you should do it, and I was feeling pretty loose and chilled and everything, so I said yeah and okay. I don't know why but it seemed like a bit of a laugh and that.

So Letisha says to use her bedroom cos there's a dressing table and a mirror so I can see what Lindsay is doing to me. But I felt like I could trust Lindsay anyway. So we went into Letisha's bedroom.

We just had the bedside lamp on and Lindsay lit three candles on the dressing table. I just sat pretty still while Lindsay did the business on me. She was really careful, and the tip of her tongue stuck out between her lips when she was concentrating. Funny that I can remember a little detail like that but it was really cute.

She put some white powder on me face and then black eyeliner and mascara and I even sat still while she put that black lipstick on me. That was the strangest part, really. I'd obviously never had lipstick on before and it felt really waxy and weird, but it didn't take long to get used to it.

I sat staring at meself in the mirror while she put black nail varnish on me fingers. We could hear the music and the odd laugh coming from the living room, but they never came in to see what we were doing. It was like they'd forgotten all about us.

We had to wait for the nail varnish to dry, so we just sat in the bedroom, talking and stuff. I was still pretty wasted with the vodka, and I kept staring at the way the candlelight sparkled on the silver bar that was pierced through Lindsay's eyebrow and wondering how much it had hurt having that done.

Then, when me nails were just about dry, Lindsay said, "Well, what do you think?"

I looked at meself in the mirror with all that black and white make up on me face and I realised that I just looked stupid.

Lindsay seemed to sense that and she said that I only looked strange because of what I was wearing, and how that just wouldn't go with the make up. She said it would be different if I was wearing clothes that went with the look.

I told her, "I can't stand the thought of having all that frilly lace next to me."

And right then, at that moment, something changed. It was like the whole world outside the room had been put on pause and me and Lindsay were the only things that were real.

She said, "Have you ever worn any lace?"

I said, "No."

And she said, "Then how can you know you won't like it."

I think I just shrugged or something. Lindsay took her jacket off, and she was wearing this black lace thing, like a vest that buttoned all the way up the front. It came down really low so I couldn't help noticing her tits and how she wasn't wearing a bra, but Lindsay didn't seem to notice me looking or mind if she did. She told me to take me shirt off, and I just laughed but I pulled off the red tee shirt with the Ferrari emblem on it while she unbuttoned that lace vest. Obviously I was staring at her tits, but she didn't care. She just handed me that black lace vest and told me to put it on. While I was buttoning it up, she put me tee shirt on, and it looked good on her, I have to say. On her, it didn't seem to matter that it didn't go with the make up, somehow.

The vest fitted me, which was a bit of a surprise, but then, like I've said, I am pretty thin. It just sagged a bit at the top of the front where usually Lindsay's tits would fill it out. And the funny thing is, I kind of liked the feel of it.

Lindsay could tell, because she said, "See, I knew you'd like it."

I looked at meself in the mirror and I liked the way the black lace went with the make up.

Lindsay said, "With that make up and the way your hair flops over your forehead, it's hard to say whether you're a boy or a girl."

I turned to tell her to fuck off, but she was laughing and I started laughing as well. It was pretty funny. And then before I knew what was happening, she was kissing me. And pulling me onto the bed. And no, we didn't get off or anything. We just lay there kissing for a few minutes. Then she said, "So you like the feel of that lace then?"

I had to say that I did, and she kissed me again.

"I'm wearing something else that's lacy. You should try it on. I'll bet you'll like it."

I asked her what it was, but she just kept smiling at me while she reached down and lifted up her skirt. And she started pulling her knickers down. And yeah, they were dead skimpy and they were made of black lace.

I said, "Oh no, I'm not doing that." But it was dead sexy watching her pull them off like that and she didn't stop.

She was hanging them on the end of her finger right in front of me face. "Go on. Put them on. See how it feels."

I asked her if the others were wearing girls' knickers and she laughed and said she didn't know. But she kept on at me to try hers on. And in the end, I did. I don't really know why. I think it must have been all that vodka. But I took me jeans off and took me boxers off, and I wasn't embarrassed like I had been getting undressed in front of me sister, even though Lindsay was watching. And I took that thong from her and I put it on.

I suppose it doesn't matter, just talking into this recorder thing, so I'll admit it; it felt really good. No, I mean it. You should try it if you don't believe me. While Lindsay put me boxers on, I got up off the bed and looked at meself in the mirror. I couldn't stop staring. With the black and white make up Lindsay had put on me, and the lacy underwear, I couldn't even recognise that it was me. And because I am so pale and thin, I realised that what Lindsay had said earlier was true. I could easily be a girl.

That was when the bedroom door opened and Letisha was standing there saying, "What's keeping you two?" And then she just stood looking at us for a few seconds. Then she burst out laughing. "Hey, come and have a look at this!" she shouted.

I said, "No! It's not what you think!" But pretty soon, everyone was piled into that bedroom and laughing and taking the piss. And after a while, even I realised that it was pretty stupid trying to cover meself up with just me hands and I started laughing as well. Cos the funny thing was, I could tell that they weren't laughing at me, if you know what I mean. They were just laughing because it was a ridiculous sight, seeing me dressed in Lindsay's undies like that.

And then Carrie said, "Hey, we should all do it." So next thing you know, everyone is swapping their undies, except for Dave, who was too zonked out with vodka and blow to really know where he was. And Danny took out his phone and started taking pictures of all of us. And we were all posing, taking the piss out of fashion models and that. And we drank some more and listened to more music. And we just had a fucking great time.

CHAPTER 6

It was way after eleven o' clock when we all piled out of Letisha's place that night. We had to walk down the stairs and some of the landings were pitch black where the lights weren't working. It was pretty tricky, cos we'd all been drinking a lot and the rest of them had been doing weed, and we virtually had to carry Dave, cos he was so wasted. But we did make it to the bottom safe enough in the end.

Outside it was cold, and there was a real fog so that you couldn't see more than twenty yards. The streetlights stood out like orange blobs just hanging there in the grey mist. It made everything seem dead quiet and even the cars sounded like they were miles away and not zooming down the dual carriageway on the edge of the estate.

Now this was my estate, remember, and none of the others lived here, so we were going to have to split up now. And you know, I was dead broken up about that inside. I remember thinking that maybe it would be cool to be a Goth and hang out with them all the time.

Josh said, "One last fag before we all head off?" and I said yeah and how I'd get some of them clove fags so we could smoke mine next time. And Dave stirred at that and said, "Who says there's going to be a next time?"

The atmosphere between us was suddenly colder than the fog and nobody said anything at first. But finally Lindsay says, "Ignore him, he's just wrecked," and everyone says yeah and what a good night it's been and that, and how we should get together again. And then Dave was sick, right there where he stood. He just bent over and puked. And while it was disgusting, we all couldn't help but laugh while we watched him.

Then the others all headed off home, and I stood and watched them. Just before they got swallowed up by the fog, Lindsay turned and waved and blew me a kiss. And it sent shivers running all through me. And then they were gone, though I could still hear their footsteps and the murmur of their voices and the occasional laugh.

I stood where I was, listening, until I couldn't hear them anymore. And then I turned and began me walk through the tower blocks, rising like black giants into the grey night air. I looked at me reflection in a shop window, beyond the shutters, and there was traces of make up, even though I thought I'd washed off the stuff that Lindsay had put on.

Lindsay. She's cute. And all I could think of was us lying on Letisha's bed, wearing each other's undies and just talking and kissing. Let me say right now, since it doesn't matter anymore, I hadn't been much of a guy with girls. I mean I like girls and all that and I ain't queer or anything. It's just that I've never had a girlfriend or nothing apart from Sharlene, and as I said that didn't end well. Loads of the other boys at school have, and when I hear them talking about what they've done, I've always been dead jealous. And especially when I see boys who've got steady girlfriends. I'd love to have a girlfriend. But I just don't know how to go about that now. I've never really known how to talk to girls like that, you know, to ask em out. I don't know what to say. And what if they say no?

But anyway, talking with Lindsay and kissing her and all that, and hanging around with all of them, it felt like I'd got some real friends. And walking back home, I can remember thinking that the way it was with Lindsay, well, that's what it must be like to have a girlfriend. A proper girlfriend.

Friends. Girlfriends. Just what the fuck was I thinking. I've never had either. And I should have known better right then. Maybe if that kid hadn't run out of the fog and banged right into me, scaring me shitless and sending both of us flying, I would have realised that. But this kid did do just that. And when we picked ourselves up, with a lot of swearing and threatening on my part, I realised that it was Jimmy Warnock, a kid who lives in our tower block a few floors lower down than us. Jimmy's twelve and he's a bit of a tear-arse and always in trouble, so me swearing and threats had no effect on him; he just stood there, facing me out.

"Where've you been?" he asked me right out. I told him it was none of his fucking business. Then he asked me if I'd got any fags. Well of course I hadn't and I told him to just go nick some off his mum and he said he'd tried but she'd caught him with the packet and smacked him on the head until he'd had to run out of the flat. His mum's a bit rough and with loads of tattoos and that, and I'd have run a mile if she was after me.

Then he must have noticed me hands, cos he points at them and says, "What's that on yer fingers? Are yer turning into a girl or summat?"

I held me hands out in front of me and looked down at them. I hadn't washed that black nail varnish off and that's what Jimmy had seen. I must have been so pissed and concentrating on getting the make up off me face that I'd forgotten all about the stuff on me nails.

I told Jimmy to fuck off, and kicked out at him so that he ran out of reach. He was just in sight in the thick fog, and he was shouting back at me, "You're a nancy boy you are. You're gay." And just like a kid, he just kept shouting it and laughing and there was no malice in it, but it was just dead annoying. And he knew that it was, because although I chased after him a couple of times, he always stayed out of reach and he kept coming back, taunting, and you could hear the laughter in his voice so you knew that, to him, this was just the best kind of fun he could think of having at this moment.

In the end, I gave up and turned to head for home. Jimmy stayed just far enough out of reach, following behind me, catcalling all the while, until he finally tired of me lack of response and he was gone, fuck knows where, into the fog and the dark. All the same, during the short walk back to our block, it made me think, what Jimmy had been saying. Not about being gay. God, I knew I wasn't a queer or anything like that. No, what I mean is, it made me think about what it had felt like, having that make up on, and wearing Lindsay's undies. I can say it here, cos like I said, nothing matters anymore. But what I ended up thinking was that it felt pretty good wearing em. And I liked how I looked when I saw meself in the mirror like that. Now I remember telling meself it was probably cos I was pissed and all that. But I can remember thinking as I got back to our block, and even as I was pressing the buttons for the lift – which in our block was working – that it felt dirty thinking like that. All the same, I couldn't stop thinking about it.

When I got to our flat, I let meself in. Bastards one and two were both on the sofa watching the telly. I could see the half empty booze bottles on the laminated coffee table in front of them and I could see the glass bong as well, so I had a fair idea what condition they were in. At least they were dressed though.

"Is that you babes?" me mum slurred out without even turning to look. The other bastard was spark out beside her but he stirred then and turned, and I suppose he must have seen me through his squinting eyes.

"Yeah," he says, "he's back."

"Come over here babes," me mum says. "Come on. I'm dead sorry for what happened. You know I wouldn't hurt yer on purpose."

Well I did walk over and stood between them and the telly and I got a kick out of being in his way and him trying to watch it around me.

"Yer know that, don't yer babe? That I wouldn't hurt yer on purpose?"

I have to say, she was dead pathetic, lying back there all stoned and pissed and I knew she was right, but all I could say was, "Well you did hurt me. That was a bastard trick."

And then he chirps up, "We'll get them tools back for yer. And we'll get some more. Promise. We'd forgot you needed em. It was just a mistake that's all."

It was like he was pleading and it was so pathetic cos I knew it was a lie, like all the others I'd had to listen to over the years. But I didn't shout at him or anything. I'd done me shouting earlier. And besides, I was still a bit pissed from all the vodka and blacks at Letisha's place, so all I did was shake me head.

Then he noticed me hands. His mouth dropped open and he was sort of pointing at them. "Have you got nail varnish on?" he asked. "Look, look at that," he says, turning to me mum. "He's got bloody nail varnish on."

"Have yer babes?" she asks in that moronic space cadet drawl. "Have you been experimenting babes, finding out who you are and that?"

What the fuck all that was about I don't know. But she does watch tons of daytime telly and all I can think is she was just coming out with bollocks she's seen on Trisha or them American shows, where all kinds of freakazoids tell their secrets to the world just for the chance of being on the telly. I must have put me hands behind me back because she says, "Don't be ashamed babes. Let me see. It's cool that you want to find yerself. Better than bottling it all up inside. C'mon, let me see."

I could feel the blood colouring me cheeks and I felt hot.

"Wot's that around yer eyes," he then chips in, and he's leaning forward to look close all of a sudden. "Bloody hell, it's eye liner. He's got bloody eye liner on!" Then the bastard is laughing. "He thinks he's Alice Cooper!"

Obviously in me pissed up state, I hadn't made a good job of taking that make up off. And he's lying there now, pointing and laughing at his own joke.

But she isn't laughing. "You know you can talk to me about it, don't yer babes?" And there's that concerned mother face, the one she likes to put on when she thinks she has to be 'caring'. "I'll even help you, you know, show you how to put your make up on and that." Well this was fucking rich since half the time she was so stoned that when she put her own on she looked like a fucking circus clown. "And if you – you know – want to try on any of me stuff, I'll always help you."

She wasn't joking either. She was dead hippy-fucking-serious about it. In that less-than-a-minute, she'd convinced herself that I was trying to be a girl. Fucking crack head bastard! What's more, it sounded like there was nothing she'd like better than for that to be true.

Then she says, "We can go shopping together if you like, I can help you choose stuff that really suits you. I still love yer babes, no matter what."

To be honest, I don't know if she said anything else because I just made a dash for me room and slammed the door behind me. I lay on top of me bed and didn't try to get undressed. And I couldn't sleep, even though when I'm pissed like that I can usually fall asleep right away. I was thinking of the whole night with Dave and Danny and Josh and Carrie and Lindsay, over at Letisha's place. Especially I was thinking about Lindsay. And then I realised that we hadn't arranged to meet up again, and I remembered what Dave had said about there not being a next time and that. But I wanted there to be a next time. So I planned on just trying to hang out with them a bit at school after the weekend. And I'd get some of them clove fags in the meantime. And if I had to be a fully-fledged

Goth, then what the fuck – it wasn't like I had any other mates to hang out with. Why the fuck not?

At the same time though – and I remember this dead clear – I was lying there and thinking how much I'd liked wearing Lindsay's undies and how I was a bit worried about how much I'd liked it. And I must have fell asleep telling meself that it had only been because I was pissed. But there was more to it than that.

CHAPTER 7

So next day was Saturday. I got up dead early as usual to go to work at the abbatoir. I scrubbed all that stuff off me nails and I was feeling like shit and probably still a bit pissed from the vodka the night before.

It was a crap day and I hate working in that place. The stink of it nearly made me chuck up a few times, with all that blood and guts and stuff, and all the foul muck that comes out of the innards, and the blokes who work there and all their filthy habits. I could never work in a place like that full time. But looking at the blood I couldn't help thinking of the night before and how Goths were into Dracula and blood and that. Blood of the Prince. Well I couldn't see how any of em would want to drink the stinking slops that washed around the floor of that place.

Still, I got through the day, with the blokes all taking the piss out of how wrecked I looked, and at least I walked out with me pay in me pocket. It was cold and already dark when I finished, but at least it wasn't raining or foggy. And I decided to walk home, through the town. It was still pretty busy cos the shops were all still open and it was like the lights were sort of calling you to come inside where it was warm and bright. I wasn't in any great mood to go home, so I wandered in and out of some of the bigger shops.

I wasn't really looking for anything, just passing time, but I found meself hanging around the make up counters. I suppose I was thinking of Lindsay and the night before. Anyway, when I realised that, I started looking at the make up. Most of it was dead girly and red and pink and that, and I wasn't really looking for that at all. I was looking for the black stuff and the purple stuff that the Goths wore. I could see it all right, but I couldn't nick any. The shops weren't busy enough and the people working there were watching out the whole time. I don't suppose I looked like I belonged, hanging out around the make up and perfume counters and that, with me scruffy work clothes on and bits of blood and stuff on me shoes, so they seemed to be keeping a close eye on me.

So in the end, I decided to head for home. All the way back to our estate, I kept thinking about Lindsay and the others and wondering what they were going to be doing that night. And I was wishing that whatever it was, I could be with them. But I didn't have their phone numbers or anything so I couldn't call them, and I dunno if I'd have rung even if I had. So I decided as far as that was concerned, I'd stick with what I'd thought of doing at first, just catching up with them at school on the Monday and seeing what happened.

So it was back to the flat and another Saturday night in on me own. At least I had the little telly and me Playstation. They were locked in the cupboard in me room, with some other stuff. It's where I should have put me tools so that they wouldn't have got at em. Served me right for being lazy, that did. But I still think they are bastards for doing what they did. And it's not like the first time they'd done it. This telly and Playstation aren't the first ones I've had, for example. They took the others just a couple of months after they'd given em to me for Christmas last year. They hadn't been new then, but they'd been just what I'd wanted and I was made up when I got em. Like I said, though, within a couple of months they'd gone, flogged on so that the bastards could buy more dope or whatever it had been. I don't think the selfish swines ever know how much it hurts me when they do things like that. It's always "We had to babes. We'll get you new ones, promise." But I'm used to knowing that they won't. It's all bollocks. The telly and Playstation I have now, I bought meself, second hand, with the money I get from the Saturday job at the abattoir.

The walk home took about half an hour from the town, and when I got back to the estate, lights were on in most of the flats in the tower blocks. I had to walk past the garages to get to my block. There's two rows of em opposite each other and a patch of tarmac in between. They're not all used now cos of the vandalism and that, and all the garage doors are covered with tags and some are kicked in. One is even burned out. They put CCTV cameras up a few months back, and the kids who do all this have just moved on. Still, a few people keep cars in these garages, the ones who nobody would dare mess with. Like Kyle.

Kyle's car is out on the tarmac in front of his garage, and Kyle is there with a few of his mates looking in under the bonnet, with one of them portable floodlight sets you can get dead cheap from Halfords where he works, lighting up the engine. Me mate Johnno – well I call him me mate, cos if I hang around with anyone, it's him, but not that often really – well he's there as well, and he sees me and calls out to me. I didn't really want to go over, cos I was supposed to be helping Kyle with his car, but without any tools all I'd be able to do is watch. Anyway, I see Kyle look up. He doesn't say anything, but I want to stay in with Kyle so I walk over to them.

Kyle says, "I thought you wanted to help with this," when I get there. "We're just cleaning the injectors now."

I have to tell him how I haven't got any tools anymore and what happened. Kyle's mates all start laughing and taking the piss, and one of them, Keith Stanway, starts saying how he's seen me mum down at the shops that morning and she looked like a fucking zombie who'd been dressed by a blind retard.

I'm not angry when he says this with all the others laughing and that, but what I do feel is dead embarrassed and ashamed.

Kyle turns to them and says, "Fucking leave it out. That's out of fucking order," and they all shut up. They all do what Kyle tells em. I hadn't expected Kyle to jump in like that. He's not always like that. He could have just as easily started taking the piss along with them. But I was glad he was in one of his good moods then. So I did end up working on that engine for a bit, holding parts and passing tools while they worked, and although I was dead tired from having a hangover all day and being at work and that, I stuck around until it was all finished.

Before I went, Kyle asked me about me sister. He said he'd seen her with the baby that morning and she was looking good. I could only think that she'd made a special effort for some reason, cos like I said, I think she's let herself go a bit since she had the baby and got her own flat. Loads of her stuff is still in me room, in a chest of drawers and there's a few bits still hanging in the wardrobe. She keeps saying she's going to come and pick them up, but she never does. Anyway I thought it was interesting, Kyle asking after her, cos they used to go out for a bit, back when Kyle was still at school. I can remember thinking that it would be dead cool if they started going out again, like it would mean that I could start hanging out with Kyle or something. As if. Still, it gave me something to think about as I walked back to the tower block.

When I did get home, there was nobody in. They were probably round at some of their friends, doing some crap or other or boozing. The flat was all dark, so I put all the lights on. I was a bit hungry, so I started hunting around the kitchen and in the fridge. There wasn't much there, but I found enough to do some cheese on toast, and I took it back to me room. When I put the light on, it was obvious right away that she'd been in there. There was some stuff on the bed. Make up. It was all brand fucking new as well, so she'd been out and bought it. Or nicked it. All fucking pink and red it was as well; nail varnish and powder and lipstick and stuff, and mascara and eye liner. I'd hoped she'd been so stoned that she wouldn't have remembered about the night before but it was just like her to remember this. I picked this stuff up and looked at it all and I just felt sick. And how typical that they don't think twice about taking me tools, the things that really can make me what I want to be, but think they're doing me a favour getting me stuff they think I need cos they think I want to be a girl. I just swiped all that stuff off the bed and onto the floor. And I lay down and I didn't even think of getting me Playstation out cos actually, I just felt sick.

CHAPTER 8

I woke up early on the Sunday morning. About six o'clock. It was cold in me room so I didn't really want to get out of bed, but I made meself do it all the same. In the end, I'd had to, cos I was dying for a slash and I'd been holding it in until I was starting to burst. I only put the light on when I came back from the bathroom and straightaway I saw it all there on the floor. All that make up, I mean. I picked it all up and stacked it on the dressing table, which was still full of lots of me sister's stuff. It was like I couldn't bring meself to throw it away, with it all being brand new and in shiny packaging and that. And anyway, while I was holding these lipsticks and mascaras and things, it all got me thinking about what it had been like on the Friday night over at Letisha's place. And I was thinking about how cool it was when Lindsay was putting that Goth make up on me in Letisha's bedroom. And it was funny really, cos sitting there, when I wasn't pissed at all, I realised how much I'd enjoyed it all. Being with Lindsay and that crowd, having her put that dark make up on me. It made me feel like I was starting to belong.

They'd all said that I'd make a good Goth cos of how I'd looked and I remember I'd thought what a load of bollocks that all was. But thinking back, I could see that it didn't matter whether they were just talking out of their arses or not; what mattered was whether or not I felt that I wanted to become a Goth. And the funny thing was, I could see that I really did want that. I didn't know why, to be honest, and I started trying to think why I was feeling this way. I knew what it would mean for me to become a Goth; I'd seen what it was like for them. People staring all the time; people making stupid comments behind their backs; people

taking the piss – especially kids. Why the
fuck would I want to put myself through all
that? But thing was, I really did feel that
I wanted it. Maybe it's because I'd never
really had a gang of real friends. And it
had felt really good being with them, being
accepted by them, and just having a great
time hanging out. That must have been
part of it, I'm sure of it. I'd never realised
just how lonely I was a lot of the time until
that Friday night when I'd been out with
them. And right there, sitting on me bed
last Sunday, on me own, well that's when I
did realise it. And I didn't want to be always
on me own anymore.

But there was more to it than that.
There was Lindsay as well. She'd been dead
kind to me and I had to admit, the more
I'd thought about her the more I'd fancied
her. I sat there thinking of her in Letisha's
bedroom. On Friday night, when I'd first
seen her, I said that she would look dead
good without all that Goth make up – the
black lipstick and white powder and all
that. But sitting on me bed thinking about
her then, I could feel that I just fancied her

loads, and even with the Goth make up and all them black clothes and that. I fancied her just as she was. I was wondering if she fancied me as well, remembering how gentle and careful she'd been putting that make up on me face. And then how we'd been lying on Letisha's bed, just talking. And kissing. I told meself, it must have just been the drink and the blow she'd been smoking. But as I held a packet of the pale-pink lipstick that me stupid crack head mother had put in me room, I remembered the waxy feel of that black lipstick that Lindsay had put on me. And how it felt, kissing her while I was wearing it. And I couldn't help remembering what it had felt like when she'd made me put on that black lacy vest of hers and how that felt against me skin. And how it had gone further; how she'd got me to wear her little black thong. And how I hadn't minded then, and how I didn't feel stupid about it now. It had been new. It had been . . . well, kind of exciting if you must know. And it had been with Lindsay. In fact it was all new and kind of exciting. Vodka and black becoming the "Blood of the Prince", wearing the clothes, listening to that dark music and all that. And I knew it right then. I knew it for certain. I wanted to be part of it all. I wanted to become a Goth.

I picked up the make up from the dresser. There was nothing I could really use, cos it was all too girly and pink and that. But I'd have to get some of me own. And I'd have to get the gear as well. I'd have to dress the part if I was going to hang out with Lindsay and Josh and Dave and them. Well I had a bit of money, and I wasn't going to need it for the mechanic course anymore. So I thought I might as well go shopping. I wondered where I'd find all of that black gear. I'd just have to look around all the shops. Everything they wore seemed to be black. Even Lindsay's thong. Funny how I kept coming back to thinking of that. How good it had felt putting it on and feeling it next to my skin, just lying there with Lindsay.

That was when I started to wonder about meself, if I'm honest. Cos I found meself looking at the chest of drawers that still had loads of me sister's stuff in it. And I was wondering if she had a black lacy thong in there.

Well, I never looked in me sister's chest of drawers right then, in case that's what you're thinking. Actually, I just got dressed and went and sat in the living room. I could hear snoring from their room, so I knew that they were back and that they probably wouldn't be surfacing till sometime in the afternoon. So I just watched the telly and waited until it was time for the shops to open. They all opened later on Sundays, so I had to hang around for quite a while, with all nervous thoughts running through me head, like what would happen if they didn't want me to be a Goth with them. What if Lindsay wasn't interested in me – which I convinced meself was more and more likely. But then I told meself that it didn't matter if Lindsay wasn't interested in me. I mean, I would rather that she was and everything, but even if she wasn't, it would be dead cool just hanging out with them and being a part of what they were part of. That's what

I really wanted more than anything. I was sick of being on me own all the time. And I was sick of that snoring pair of thieving bastards down the hall. Why shouldn't I make a life of me own?

So later that morning – well, nearer dinner time actually – I found meself in the centre of town. Most of the shops are the same as you'd find in any town centre and they all look grimy somehow, from the outside at any rate. But in the centre of our town, there's this dead little winding alleyway. There are these dead small shops hidden away down there; like there's this dressmaker's shop and this shop that makes and sells small sports trophies and that. Pretty specialist, and you can tell that they've all been there pretty much forever. But one of these shops is a tobacconist, and when you go in there's this smell of tobacco and cigars and stuff, and it's actually quite nice. I'd never been in that shop before, but I'd been past it loads of times. I did go in then though, and there was this little bell that rang when I opened the door. It was dark in that shop, but it was warm. An old bloke came out from the back somewhere and asked me what I wanted. I told him I was after some clove cigarettes and I half expected him to ask me what I was talking about, but he just turned to the shelf behind him and took down a pack that seemed to look like the ones we'd been smoking on the Friday night. They were dead expensive compared to normal fags, but I bought them anyway, and a cheap black lighter.

I was going to save them until Monday, when I'd see Lindsay and Josh and them at school. But out in the square, with all the people milling about and wrapped up against the cold, I just couldn't resist it. I took one of the fags from the packet and lit it. I almost coughed me lungs up right away; I'd forgotten how strong and dry they were. But after a bit, I was enjoying smoking away, and I was thinking about what I'd say next day at school. I mean, do you just go up to them and say, "I've decided to be a Goth like you"? I mean, that sounds a bit crap. And I was wondering just what I had to do to get to hang around with them. Do I ask them if they'd mind, right out like that? What if they said no? Do I just sort of hang around with them anyway and hope that I sort of just become one of their gang over time? It was amazing what a big deal it all seemed to me. One thing was for sure, I could never be so divvy as to come right out with stuff like that. And in the end, what I decided was, when I saw them at school, I'd go over and say hi, and offer around the fags, cos I'd smoked all theirs on the Friday like. And while we were talking and smoking and that, I'd ask Lindsay if she'd teach me how to do me own make up and that. I'd have some with me. And that would kind of tell em that I was interested in becoming one of them, doing it bit by bit. And that seemed like a really good idea to me. I could picture it all in me head. But I was going to need some make up. And that was one of the reasons I'd come into town in the first place.

I had money in me pocket, sure, but I wasn't going to spend it unless I really had to. I'd got me big quilted jacket on with deep pockets, so you know what I'm talking about. I went into all the shops and they were getting quite busy by dinner time. It was dark and cloudy outside but in the big shops it was warm and dead light, so that's where people were. I wandered around a few of the big places like Boots and Debenhams and Superdrug and that, where they have tons of make up and stuff. Debenhams was definitely out, cos the way they have the make up is it's all behind these counters and there's girls behind the counters wearing white coats like they're lab technicians or something. I recognised some of the girls from school, there doing weekend jobs. So I got everything I needed from other places where they had stuff out on shelves, like, and you could just walk around and pick stuff up and look at it. And stuff it in your pocket if you had the nerve and knew what you were doing. The only thing I ended up paying for was a Kohl pencil. I bought a Maybelline one from Boots. To tell the truth, I didn't much know what it was I was getting, but I ended up with black and purple lipsticks and mascaras and this white powder and that, and I hadn't got a clue how to use it. Oh, and one other thing I bought was this black jacket. It was in the Oxfam shop but I saw it from the street so I went in and had a look. It was black and it had these straps and buckles on it and it was a bit big for me, but I thought it looked good anyway, so I got it. It only cost me a fiver.

When I got home, I chucked all the stuff on me bed and I lay down there meself, holding it and looking at it. I had another one of the clove fags I'd bought as well, and I was thinking of Lindsay. And I kept wondering about how good that lacy stuff felt when she made me wear it. She said she didn't know if the other lads wore lacy underwear and stuff next to their skin, but I was betting that they did, like. Cos it felt so cool and the way Lindsay suggested that I try it, I reckoned that it was something she'd done before. I was betting it was something they all did.

And I found I kept looking over at that dresser where there was still loads of me sister's stuff that she hadn't taken over to her flat yet. I stubbed me fag out in the ashtray on the floor and walked over to the dresser. I was wondering if me sister had any lacy black thongs that she'd left in there. Or a lacy vest or something. Well there was only one way to find out, so I started opening the drawers.

In the bottom drawer, there were just jumpers and stuff, and I saw the one that I'd nicked and given her for her birthday. She'd said she'd really liked it, but come to think of it, I'd never seen her wearing it. She'd just stuffed it in here all the time. The cow. Not that I minded really – it's not like I'd saved up and paid for it or anything. In the next drawer up there was all summer T-shirts and shorts and that, stuff she would definitely not be needing at this time of year. I was beginning to think I wouldn't find anything I was after, but just like you'd guess, the last drawer I looked in – the top drawer – was full of underwear. Mind you, I couldn't see anything that looked black in there. There was loads of thongs and that, and some of em were dead flimsy and lacy just like Lindsay's were, but none of them were black. Some were white and some were pink and some were red, and some had, like, these little bows embroidered on em. And some had little roses on them and that. And there were matching bras and that, and stockings and tights and stuff and even suspender belts. But I couldn't see anything black, except for the stockings. My sis obviously didn't go for black undies – unless she'd taken all the black ones with her.

I dunno why, but I started to take the thongs out of the drawer and laid them on me bed. Even just holding em in my hands and running me fingers across them, I was reminded of what it had felt like to touch Lindsay's. If I closed me eyes, I didn't have to see that they were all pink and girlie and that. I could imagine that they were all black, and that I was back in Letisha's flat with Lindsay, lying on the bed and hearing the Goth music and the laughter of the others from the next room. That had been the best night of me whole life. I absolutely knew it. And so, with me eyes still closed, I took off me trousers and me pants and I put on one of me sister's thongs. And that was how I fell asleep and I didn't wake up until the next morning, which shows how knackered I must have been.

CHAPTER 9

Shit. It's really dark outside now. And the fog outside is dead thick. I can just about see other buildings – the ones nearby – but I can't see the tower block where me sister lives. That's how thick it is. And it's dark here in me room without any lights on. It's funny the way that you can see these orange blobs. You know that they are streetlights, but all you get is this orange glow in the grey fog. And then you see yellow blobs, moving, and you know that they are car headlights but they look like they could be alien space probes or something. That's what I like to think, anyway. Even if I know that it's just people in their cars. People just going about their business. Living each day as it comes.

People like Kyle and that. People who still have things to look forward to.

So . . . I got to school early on the Monday. I suppose I was hoping to see them all. So I hung around by the bike sheds where I could have a smoke and could keep an eye on the gates, right up until the bell went. None of them had showed up by then. So I went inside to me class and I must admit I felt a bit let down, like. It was like I'd been building it all up inside me head, what it would be like to see em all. And another thing is, I'd been a bit nervous as well. While I was sitting at me desk in the classroom, I realised that what I'd been nervous about was that they might not want to have anything to do with me. That had been at the back of my mind all over the weekend as well. What I kept thinking about was the way that Dave had said, "Who says there's going to be a next time?" as we were going our own ways at the end of the night. I know that what I should have been thinking about was how everyone else had been all for it and that, and how we'd all had a dead good time and lots of laughs and that. But all I kept thinking about was what Dave had said. And then I'd been thinking about all kinds of stuff, like how they would all have been together over the weekend, and how they might have all changed their minds about me or they might not have ever meant any of it in the first place. We'd all been totally pissed, after all. All kinds of shit like that went through me head.

Anyway, before our class teacher arrived, Mr Keane, Josh rolled up, and the first thing he did when he walked in the classroom was wave over at me. I can't tell you how good it felt seeing him do that. I waved back and he walked over to my desk.

He said, "Good night on Friday, over at Letisha's?"

I told him, "Yeah, it was." It was all sounding pretty good so far.

Then he laughed and said, "You should have seen yourself in all that make up Lindsay put on yer. I bet yer felt a right divvy."

I told him that I had been too pissed to care, really, and he said it wouldn't have mattered if I hadn't been, cos Lindsay can be dead persuasive and she always gets her own way in the end. I laughed at that as well but I didn't tell him that Lindsay wouldn't have to be too persuasive to get me to do anything she wanted.

Then Josh said, "Actually, you looked pretty good really. You'd make a dead good Goth, like we was saying."

I wondered then, if he was sort of asking me if I wanted to join them. I know that sounds stupid, like I'm making it sound like they were some sort of club or something, with membership cards and all, but I don't know how else to put it. You know what I mean though. In the end, I just said, "Yeah, I've been thinking about that meself." And I opened me bag and showed him the make up I'd nicked the day before.

He said, "Bloody hell, it didn't take you long to get hooked."

I said, "Thing is, I don't even know how to put it on. I'm going to need lessons." I laughed when I said that and he laughed as well, and said, "It's not that hard once you get used to it. You should get Lindsay to show you again."

Well of course that's exactly what I had in mind, but I didn't tell him that.

"You coming for a fag at break time?" he asked, and I said, "Yeah," and that I'd even got some clove fags.

He nodded then and said, "See yer at break then," and went to sit at his usual desk.

Well I can't remember a word of what was said in them first two lessons cos all I was doing was sitting waiting for the bell to ring for break time. And when it did, Josh beckoned over to me, and off we went to the bike sheds to meet the others.

I was disappointed when I got there; Lindsay wasn't there. I tried not to show it though, and passed the clove fags around. Josh said what a good night it had been round at Letisha's on Friday, and Danny started laughing and said I should have seen myself in that make up that Lindsay had put on me and I said that I had seen meself in the mirror and that. Carrie said that I'd looked dead good, and really wasted, and how Lindsay ought to get a job as a make up artist for films and that cos she was so good with it.

Then Josh said, "He's got a load of make up of his own with him," and Carrie said, "Have you really?" and, "Why aren't you wearing any?"

She was looking at Josh and Danny and Dave cos they were all wearing eyeliner at least, and Josh even had black nail varnish on.

I had to tell them that I didn't know how to put it on and that I was hoping that Lindsay would be able to show me.

"She's not come in today," Carrie said, and Danny said she'd got a bit of a headache.

"She's still stoned from last night most likely," Dave said. It was the first thing he'd said, and he hadn't smiled either.

Carrie said, "She wasn't that wrecked. She's just got a migraine that's all."

There was something funny about Dave – he wasn't being as friendly as the others, but at the time I didn't pay much attention, cos all I could think about was how they must have been out together last night having a good time and that, while I was at home on me own.

Anyway, Carrie says, "I can show you how to put some eyeliner on if you want."

I said, "All right," and how that would be great, but I really wanted Lindsay, and it must have showed, cos Carrie said, "And I can give you Lindsay's phone number if you want. You can call her tonight and I bet she'd be dead glad to show you how to put make up on properly. She loves doing that and she's dead into it."

And Dave said, "So yer want to become an instant Goth then do yer?" and the way he said it, it was like it was not meant to be nice or anything.

The others turned on him and told him to shut his mouth and that I was all right and that, and I have to say that I was dead pleased, cos it seemed that apart from Dave, they all wanted me to hang out with them. All the worrying and planning I'd been doing over the weekend had been just a waste of time.

Anyway, I arranged to meet Carrie at dinner time and she'd show me how to put on the eyeliner, saying she'd leave the rest for Lindsay to show me. And when we were walking back to class together, Josh said, "Don't pay any attention to Dave. He used to go out with Lindsay and he still gets a bit jealous when he sees her having a good time that doesn't involve him. He'll be all right once he's used to having you around."

Well that actually made me feel even better if you know what I mean. Cos it meant that Dave hadn't got anything against me hanging out with them all. It was just because I was getting on well with Lindsay. Of course, I didn't know just how much of a bastard he could be, then.

CHAPTER 10

When I got home from school, the bastards were sitting in front of the telly. They were both smoking, but only fags. And then – hold on, the fucking light's flashing on this recorder thing. The batteries are running out. I'll have to change them.

Shit that was fiddly, changing them batteries with one hand, standing up here on this wobbly chair. Now what was I saying? Oh yeah, I'd got home from school. Me mum said, "Have a good day at school babes?" but she didn't even look up from the telly.

I lit one of me own fags and just stood there looking at them. I said, "I don't suppose there's anything for tea is there?" Obviously I wasn't expecting there to be anything cos the lazy bastards had never done anything like that for years. Me and me sister had been looking after ourselves since way back. I was just saying it to wind them up. I wasn't even hungry.

Me dad did notice the smell of me clove fag though, and he looked up and said, "Bloody hell, what's that you're smoking?" And then he noticed the black eyeliner round me eyes and the black nail varnish on me fingers and he started laughing and said, "Hey up, he's wearing make up again."

Me stupid mother turned and looked then and said, "Oh did yer like that stuff I got yer babes?"

You know, I didn't even say anything. I just turned and went to me room. And lying on me bed, I picked up me phone and I called Lindsay. Normally I'd have been dead nervous about doing something like that, but hanging out with the others at school and that had made me feel good and so I just phoned.

Lindsay was dead cool and we talked for about twenty minutes. And the thing was, she said I should go round to her place later and bring the make up and stuff with me and she'd show me how to use it. You can imagine, I was well made up when I heard this.

At about seven o' clock, I went round to her place. It was dark and it was foggy again, but I didn't care. It took me about half an hour to walk over to the estate where she lived, and I had to phone her again to ask for directions to her street, but it didn't take long to find it.

When I got there, her mum and dad had gone out and there was just her and her younger sister in the house. I asked Lindsay how her headache was and she just laughed and said she hadn't had one; she just hadn't felt like going in today. I just smiled and nodded and told her that I felt like that on most days. Anyway, I was wearing that jacket – the one I'd bought from the Oxfam shop – and Lindsay said it looked really cool. Funny thing was, she didn't look all that Goth at all. I mean she still had some dark make up on, but not much – just some eyeliner and this sort of light purple lipstick and some nail varnish. But she wasn't wearing any Goth gear or that. In fact, she was wearing these pink sweatpants and a matching sweatshirt and there were rabbits embroidered on them, so that I finally twigged that they were actually pyjamas. So I said, "Is that what vampires sleep in then?"

She just giggled and looked dead cute and said, "When they're feeling the cold they do, yeah." Not that it was cold mind. It was absolutely boiling in that house, the heating was turned up that high.

Anyway, we left her sister watching the telly, and we went to her room. It was dark and black and purple, just like Letisha's flat had been. There was posters on the walls and the only ones I recognised were Marilyn Manson and Dracula. The Dracula poster was from a dead old film and I don't know the name of the actor – as if I cared anyway. So me and Lindsay spent the next few hours listening to music and smoking what was left of me clove fags and she showed me how to put on a make up base and put on powder so that me cheekbones stood out and I'd look even thinner and wasted. And she showed me how to make these dark shadows under me eyes and that, and how to put lipstick on, and I didn't know there was so much to it. Even putting the lipstick on, she used this dead thin brush to define the edges, and then she used another brush to put the lipstick on. I have to say it looked a dead professional job but I had to tell her I could never do that meself, never in a million years. Lindsay laughed and said that if we were ever going out to see a band or to a party or anything, that she would do me make up for me. And yes, obviously I picked up on that; she was talking like we'd be hanging out together. I mean, even if not just me and her, that I would be part of her crowd from now on, with Josh and Danny and Carrie. And Dave. And then she took all the make up off me and showed me how

I could put it on meself, just simple ways of doing it that even I could manage. And by the end of the night, I must admit, I'd got pretty good at it.

We'd been doing some drinking while we were sitting there in her bedroom and when I was walking home later, I was pleasantly pissed. Lindsay had given me a couple of fags to be getting on with, cos like I said, we'd smoked the last of my clove ones. So I was strolling back, between the tower blocks and the mist was so thick that I could barely see more than twenty yards in front of me. But I knew where I was going and I was thinking that for the first time in ages I was actually happy. I hadn't realised how generally unhappy I must have been until I'd had this feeling to show me. And I thought that for once, I was just looking forward to the next day and that the future might not have to be bleak after all. It was a dead good feeling as well.

Anyway, when I got back to our flat, the bastards weren't in and it was freezing, cos the heating wasn't on. I went into their room and nicked this little electric fan heater they had – selfish bastards – and took it to my room.

I must have been drunker than I thought, cos lying in bed, I could feel the room starting to go round in circles and I had to fight the feeling of wanting to throw up. Well I managed it, and I didn't chuck. But lying there, I found meself thinking. About how it felt having make up on and that, and how much I really liked it. And I got to wondering if the other lads – Josh and Danny and Dave – felt like that, or if they just wore it cos that's what you had to do to be a Goth. I'd washed off all the make up that I'd put on at Lindsay's, but now I just wanted to be wearing it again. And I was so pissed-drunk that I decided to get up and practise putting some on again. Only when I got up, I realised that I had left all my stuff at Lindsay's. I fell back onto the bed, and the room started spinning again. And then I spotted all that stuff on the dressing table. That stuff that me crack whore mother had left for me. And while it wasn't Dark and Goth, well, it wouldn't hurt to practise with it, would it? That's what I told meself. And who would see? So there I was, sitting in front of the mirror. And not really feeling pissed any more cos I was concentrating on putting on that make up. And I took me time over it and did everything the way that Lindsay had showed me. And when I was finished, I just lit a last fag and sat in front of that dressing table mirror, looking at meself. And the first thing that struck me was something they'd all been saying over at Letisha's when we were all drunk; how much I could look like a girl. Because looking at myself in the mirror then, I did look like a girl. And I could see that I was even pretty. And I didn't feel weird at all admitting that to myself.

I took the chair I was sitting on over to the window and sat looking down at the fog and the blobs of orange streetlights below. And I blew smoke at the glass, watching it spread slowly and stared at my reflection which seemed as though it was not me at all, but someone on the outside hanging in the mist, quietly watching me. This was when I found myself remembering what it had been like wearing Lindsay's thong and that lacy black vest. And I was sitting there, wondering what it was like to be a girl.

I can't remember doing it, but I must have opened the drawers with me sister's stuff in them. Because I was sitting back in front of the dressing table mirror, and what I was looking at didn't shock me at all. But perhaps it should have done. Cos I was wearing this pink vest and under it one of me sister's bras. And I had on this matching pink thong of hers, with little roses embroidered on it. And I was wearing these black stockings. And I stood up and looked at meself in that mirror for such a long time, turning and watching meself from different angles. And I knew that I felt good dressed like that and with the pink girlie make up on. And I felt a bit guilty, a bit dirty if you like. But the good feeling was stronger than the dirty feeling. And anyway, I wasn't doing anything wrong, was I? I wasn't hurting no one, was I? And one thing was for certain. I looked hot as a girl. Really hot. Realising that was when I started to feel guilty and dirty again. I remember taking one last look at myself in that mirror before I collapsed, pissed, onto the bed. God I looked hot.

CHAPTER 11

Well I didn't look so hot when I woke up next morning. I was still wearing my sister's gear and all me make up was smudged and that. And when I saw meself in the mirror, I felt like I must be a right pervert or something. Anyway, I took the clothes off right away and I went and had a shower and washed all that old make up off as well. By the time I got back to me room, I wasn't feeling so bad. I had been pissed, after all and we all do daft things when we're pissed, right?

Well anyway, I went to school and Lindsay was there and I hung around with her and Carrie and Josh and Danny and

Dave. And even Dave didn't seem to mind me being there, so I started to think that it was like Josh said it would be, that he was getting used to me hanging around.

Lindsay asked me why I wasn't wearing any make up. She was only joking, like, but I had to lie and say I still didn't feel confident enough to put it on meself. The truth was, that morning, I hadn't felt like putting any on. I still felt dead guilty and dirty for dressing up in me sister's stuff the night before. Cos I knew that that had had nothing to do with being a Goth. It had been about being a girl. And I was having mixed feelings about that. Because the thing is, while I felt that it was wrong and dirty, I knew that deep inside I'd liked it and wanted to do it again.

Anyway, I let Lindsay put some eyeliner on me and we all hung out together at break times and dinner time and that. And we all agreed to meet up that night at Carrie's place cos her mum and dad were going to be out. I felt that I was starting to belong. They dared me to put a full set of make up on and go to Carrie's wearing it, and I said I'd dare, but it would be my turn to dare them to do something next if I did it. I hadn't got anything in mind, but I knew I'd think of something. And I had intended to go through with it, you know. I would have done it. But of course, I hadn't counted on the bastards.

When I got home, the police were in the living room of our flat, two of them, a bloke and this woman cop. The bastards – my olds I mean, not the cops – were just sitting on the settee looking glum and nervous but not spaced out, so I knew that there was something serious going on. And you won't believe this, but the pigs were there because somebody had been dealing Es to kids at my school. And cos my bastards had previous for doing shit like that, they'd come around to our place. And they'd been waiting for me to come home cos they wanted to search the whole flat. And in particular they wanted to search my room.

Right away I felt that something was happening. I could tell by the way the bastards couldn't even look at me. The cops asked if I had any objection to them looking in my room, and I could hardly say no, so they went in. I watched them as they looked in every drawer, even the ones with me sister's clothes and that. And they picked up that girlie make up me stupid mother had got me, and they just had to make their stupid comments and that, and I just stood there watching and not saying anything. I opened the locked cupboard for them so they could check in there. But when the woman cop looked under the bed, I saw her reach deep under there and me blood went cold. I could hardly believe it when her hand came out with a bag of tabs and I knew right away what had happened. The bastards. They'd stitched me up again. They'd seen the pigs arriving or somebody had phoned to tell them, and they'd fucking well gone and hidden their stash in my room. Fucking bastards had planted it on me, their own kid! They'd been dirty and mean and neglectful all me life, but that took the cake. I told the cops that they weren't mine, that I never touched anything like that and they could check and find out I'd never been pulled in for anything. I even told them that it must have been the bastards that had planted the stuff in me room, but they wouldn't listen. They took me down the police station and they kept me there for hours and they were questioning me all the time, trying to get me to say that the gear was mine and that I'd been selling it at school and that, and where did I get it from. I kept telling them that it had nothing to do with me and that it was the bastards who'd planted it on me. And all the time, me crack whore mother was in the room telling me that it would be better for me to tell the truth and that. If there hadn't been cops there I swear I would have battered her fucking head in.

Anyway, after a few hours of it all, they charged me with possession. There had only been a few tabs in that bag, not enough for them to charge me with supplying so they let me go home on police bail, and I had to report to the police station every week until a date was set for a magistrate's hearing.

I didn't speak to me bastard mother all the way home in the taxi. Nor in the lift up to our flat. And I think she was a bit ashamed as well, cos she didn't say anything either.

When we got back, he was sitting watching the telly like he hadn't got a care in the world. She just went and sat down next to him, and I was left standing, staring at the both of them.

After a bit, she looked up at me. She said, "We had to babes. You understand, don't yer? We've both got previous, you know that. It would have been a spell inside if they'd pinned it on us, even just for possession. Yer know we wouldn't have done it if we hadn't had to. Don't yer? And yer got off lucky, didn't yer? Just a possession charge. You'll only get a slap on the wrist for that." And she smiled. And that's when I spat right in her face. And he turned to say something but I raised my hand and he thought better of it. And I would have killed him, I fucking know I would.

Instead, I just stormed off to me room and slammed the door. Of all the dirty low-down lousy tricks. I wanted to scream and

I wanted to cry. I'd never been done for anything and now I was going to have a drugs charge against me name. Of all the things I'd done wrong, like nicking stuff and that, I hadn't ever even been caught, but if I had, I'd have had to accept it, I suppose. But to get a drugs charge against me, when I had never ever touched so much as a spliff and hated the stuff cos of having to live with them and seeing what it did to them, well that was more than I could bear. And right then I hated being me, and I hated my life more than I'd ever done before. And lying on me bed, feeling all this anger, that's when I remembered that I should have gone over to Carrie's that night and hung out with Lindsay and them. And it was way too late now. And that's when I started crying. That's what the bastards had done to me. They'd taken away me dream of going on the mechanic course, and now they'd taken away the new life I was making for meself with me new friends. What would they think of me now?

I wanted to be somebody else. I just wished I could be somebody else right then.

Anybody. And I wiped away the tears and pushed back the sobs. And I sat at the dressing table. And it wasn't my Goth make up that I put on. It was the pink and red girlie stuff. And I went through me sister's clothes. And I got dressed up in her underwear and stockings and a silk top I found and this short skirt that I could remember her buying and dressed like that, and looking at meself in the mirror, I didn't feel guilty or dirty; I just felt contented. Cos it wasn't me anymore. I had become somebody else. That was a girl looking back at me in the mirror. Where I had gone I couldn't tell you. Down to hell, for all it mattered.

CHAPTER 12

I went to school the next day, and of course I saw them all and of course they were all asking why I hadn't turned up the night before. I told them the truth about what had happened and they were all dead sympathetic. They knew what kind of bastards my olds were and they knew I wasn't lying when I said that gear wasn't mine cos they knew I wouldn't even touch a spliff or anything, let alone deal anything. Even Dave seemed to think I'd had a rough deal. But he did go quiet when Lindsay said I should go over to her place that night and we could sit in her room and smoke fags and listen to music and just hang out. She said it would be better for me than staying in the flat with the bastards.

And actually, for the next week, everything went OK. I was hanging around with me new friends and I was becoming accepted and everything, and despite the fact that I had this charge hanging over me, I was starting to feel pretty good. It was an unusual feeling for me. I'd got more black clothing and this purple waistcoat from another charity shop, and I was starting to fit in more, especially as I was getting good with the make up as well. It was only at home in the flat, whether the bastards were in or not, that I felt like there was a big weight on me. And that's when I would sit at the dressing table and turn meself into the girl that was not me but somebody else. And I was growing to love the way it felt, dressed as her, with her make up on. So that I took to becoming her more and more. And I found myself wanting more and different clothes for her than I could find in me sister's drawers.

But then it all had to go wrong didn't it, like it always does for me. I took the day off school on the Tuesday just gone. I just didn't feel like going in. On the Monday, I'd got a letter telling me that a date had been set for the magistrate's hearing about the drug shit that the bastards had pinned on me. That made me feel really down and on the Tuesday, when I woke up, I just didn't feel like facing up to anyone. So I stayed home and in me room, I sat in front of the dressing table mirror for ages becoming that girl. Just the feel of slipping into those stockings and me sister's undies and wearing a skirt and a nice top, and taking me time putting on the make up, was enough to make me feel better. And then I spent hours just looking at meself, and standing up and walking around and that. And I wished that I could go out like that, just be this girl whenever I wanted to. But I knew that that could never be.

That afternoon, Lindsay called me after school. She was just checking up on me. I told her about the court hearing and how I just hadn't felt like coming in, and she said I should go round to her place that night. Well I did and we smoked and we drank some vodka and black – the blood of the prince – cos she had a bottle of vodka hidden under her bed. And we got to talking about that first Friday night we'd got together, when we went to Letisha's place. And Lindsay started saying about what a laugh it had been seeing how stiff and tense I'd been when she'd been putting make up on me for the first time. And what a laugh it had been when we'd swapped undies and everyone had piled in and seen us and laughed and then they'd all done it too. And Lindsay said it was amazing how good I was at putting me own make up on now.

I can't remember exactly how it happened, but it must have been because we were a bit pissed, like, but I ended up telling Lindsay about the girl. About how I'd been using girlie make up and dressing in me sister's clothes. Right away I wished I hadn't told her and I was waiting for her to piss herself laughing and all kinds of thoughts were racing through me head about how she'd tell everybody and what that would mean. But actually, she was amazing. She just kept saying how she'd love to see me dressed as a girl, and how I had the features and the bone structure for it and how she reckoned I'd be dead pretty. It wasn't at all what I was expecting. Anyway, bit by bit, I found myself talking about it, and saying how when I was this girl, it was like being a different person, like I was someone without a care. I told her I'd like to get more clothes though – clothes that would be me own. It's funny, it just became very easy talking to Lindsay about it all. She just thought it was dead natural somehow. And she said we should bunk off school the next day and go shopping and that she'd help me pick stuff out. And I said OK. I probably shouldn't have, but I doubt that things would have turned out any different, even if I hadn't. It was all bound to happen sooner or later. Like I've said before, it's shit being me. It always has been.

CHAPTER 13

God this is itching around me neck. It's nylon and it should be smooth, but there are bits of it sticking out and it itches like hell. And I can feel it every time I move, cos it's anchored to the top of the bunk bed. Still, it is only an old tow rope. I suppose I could tuck me chiffon scarf under it. Hold on a minute.

There, that's a bit better. Anyway, we went shopping, and one thing I found out right away was that Lindsay wasn't like me; she'd never nicked anything in her life. She seemed a bit shocked when I suggested it and that. I should have left it at that and we should have just bought stuff that we could afford. But I had to start acting the big shot didn't I? And I suppose after she'd taught me about make up and that, I felt I had to show her something that I was good at. Well I won't bore you to death with telling you what a good day we were having. I'll just tell you this bit quick, cos I'm ashamed of it. I taught Lindsay how to rob things from shops. Little stuff like accessories. And even this scarf I'm wearing now. I showed her how to palm them and slip them into her bag. And you could see she was getting excited about it, even though she felt a bit guilty and that. But in this one shop, I saw stuff that I liked but there was this woman who I recognised. I knew she was a store detective and she'd always kept a close eye on me whenever I'd been into this shop. But I really wanted this top. And when I got a chance, when Lindsay wasn't looking and when this woman was hidden from us by people, I stuffed it into Lindsay's bag without her noticing. I figured that if we got stopped going out of the shop, it would be me they would be after. But of course it didn't work like that. They stopped us both and they searched us both and they found that top in Lindsay's bag. I tried to tell them. I pleaded with them. Even though nobody believes that, I did. I fucking did! But they called the police in and Lindsay was taken to the police station. She was carrying all the other stuff we'd nicked that day as well, so it looked worse and worse. And worse than anything was, they just let me go.

Well I didn't go into school next day either. How could I? I just sat here in me room, dressed as the girl. The girl wasn't in any trouble and the girl was gorgeous. The world could be anything for her. So I sat there for hours, getting the make up and me hair just right, and putting on the stockings and the flimsy underwear and a black satin miniskirt and a white silk top. And I tried not to think of anything but being this girl until I must have been in something of a trance in front of that mirror. Cos I hadn't heard the front door of the flat being opened so the first I knew was when me bedroom door was opened. I jumped up and turned round dead shocked. And it was all dead quiet for a second, cos the two people standing just inside the door were just staring at me. It was me sister. And Kyle. They'd come around to pick up me sister's stuff.

It wasn't quiet for long. They both started pissing themselves laughing. And I didn't know where to hide. I tried to push past them but Kyle kept blocking me way. And then me sister stopped laughing and she was screaming at me and calling me a fucking pervert and trying to pull her clothes off me and that. And in the end, she just stormed out and said she didn't want any of that stuff now and how it would make her sick just to look at it. I was lying on the floor and Kyle was standing in the doorway looking down at me.

He said, "You fucking queer bastard," and I didn't say anything. I knew it wasn't worth telling him that I wasn't queer and that I only became this girl to take me away from me own horrible life.

I lay on the floor crying for quite a while after they'd gone. And that's when it hit me that everyone on the estate would know pretty soon. And worse than that, I wouldn't be working on cars with any of the boys again. They wouldn't want me around for sure. And even if they did, they would just be taking the piss all the time.

Later, I took the clothes off and washed off all the make up. There was no food in the house as usual, and no sign of the bastards either. They'd gone off somewhere, to somebody's to do the crap that they do. They didn't dare keep anything in the flat at the moment, what with the police charge hanging over me and everything. Anyway, I was hungry so I decided to go to the chippie and get something to eat. And that's when I found that word had definitely got out quick. The kids who saw me started calling me a queer and a sissy and stuff like that, throwing bricks at me, and following me and calling me names like only kids can. And you could tell that everyone else was watching and listening.

In the end, I just turned and ran back to the flat. When I got back, I just lay on me bed and started crying again. I'd never felt as down as this, even through all the shit I'd had to put up with in my life. What was I going to do? I was never going to be a mechanic now. I'd screwed up things with me new friends. And worse, I'd screwed up things for Lindsay, real bad. If it had just been that top, they might have believed that it was me to blame and that she was innocent. But it was all the other stuff in her bag as well. They'd never let it go with just a warning. My life was just shit and I wondered why I'd ever even been born.

Last night, I went out again. I was hoping that in the dark I wouldn't be noticed and there wouldn't be too many people about. I just had to get out, cos it was really getting to me just sitting in the flat. But going out was a big mistake. I saw Josh and Danny and Carrie. And Dave. They said that Lindsay's dad wasn't letting her out. Lindsay hadn't been back to school since she'd been out shopping with me. She was really messed up, Danny said. And then they all started having a go at me, saying why had I got Lindsay dragged into it, and that people from our estate were all the same and that they should have known better than to let me hang out with them. And they had heard about how I liked dressing as a girl as well. Dave said he'd always thought I was a freak. I thought that was rich, coming from them, but I didn't say anything. Then Dave just turned on me. He just started hitting me and kicking me. Carrie was screaming for him to stop, but he beat me to the ground and he jumped on top of me and just kept punching and kicking me. Josh and Danny pulled him off in the end, and I was left lying in some mud, and bleeding and crying.

Dave said, "Don't let me fucking see you again. I'll fucking kill you." And he was still shouting stuff out at me while they were walking him away.

I ran back to the flat. And the bastards were there. Fucking typical.

"What's happened, babes?" she said, but I ignored her and ran for the bathroom. I heard her saying, "Are people getting at you now they know you're different? Never mind babes, I'll always be here for you." Shit like that anyway; I wasn't really paying attention.

I lay in the bath for ages. I could wash the mud away, but me face was aching where Dave had been punching me. There was going to be bruises for sure. And there are bruises. You can still see em on me face. Or you would if I wasn't wearing this make up.

So I lay in that bath thinking that me life was over. That it wasn't worth living. And the more I thought that, the more I felt that it was true. What was there to live for now? Loads of kids were topping themselves these days. The papers said it was like an epidemic. There was even this girl from our school last year who'd taken a whole bottle of pills and killed herself. They said she had been the victim of bullying, but none of us could ever remember her being bullied particularly. Anyway, right then, it seemed like that might be a good option for me. But I couldn't take pills. I'd have to do something else. And why not? What did I have to live for? No friends, no future, no job prospects. And I was a boy who liked dressing as a girl, and that's how everybody would always see me from now on. If you live in a place like this, you'll know that labels like pervert and kiddie-fiddler will always stick. They never go away. Not that I am a kiddie-fiddler, but that's one of the things the kids were shouting at me, and that will definitely stick. My life isn't going to be worth shit anyway. So why not end it? Thinking like that, it did sound an attractive option. So here I am, dressed the way I feel most comfortable, as her, as the girl. And I'm standing on this wobbly computer chair in my room, looking down on the estate through the night time mist. There's a blue nylon towing rope around me neck and it's attached to the top of the bunk bed. All I have to do is step off. And I'll have the nerve to do it soon enough. I want to die. It's all I want. There's nothing left for me. I don't have a life.

I'm looking at me reflection in the window and it seems like the girl's face is hanging in mid air out there, hanging in the mist, looking back at me. You can see the bruises through the make up, but you can still see that she's pretty. Do I really want to kill her? But what choice do I have? There's no life here for her or me.

But hey. Maybe that's it. Maybe it doesn't have to be *here*. Why do I have to stay here? And why can't I still be a mechanic like I'd always dreamed? There's one way I might be able to do it. What about joining the army? They have great training in the army. They might take me on. And I could start a new life. Yeah. That might be a plan. I should just have a fag and think about this. Why haven't I thought about this before?

Now where are me fags? Oh yeah, on the bed there. I can just stretch over and – whoah . . . SH-I-I-I-T! . . .

If you liked Hanging in the Mist, you might like other titles in the Cutting Edge series.

The following is an extract from another Cutting Edge title. It's the first chapter of Bone Song by Sherryl Clark.

CHAPTER 1

Probably my whole class is laughing at me right now. Goody-goody Melissa McCardle in detention for three whole days after school. I bet they're dying to find out what I did to get here too, but I'm not telling.

This room is the pits. And it stinks. I mean, it really stinks. It's like two basketball teams have left all their sweaty runners in here to go mouldy, then thrown in a few banana peels and apple cores for good measure. There's one tiny window high up, and the room only fits a dozen desks.

God, I'm sitting in the front row again. Why do I do that? I thought I'd cured myself of the habit. Footsteps echo along the corridor. Two sets. There's just enough time to throw myself towards the back of the room, school bag first, and reach for a chair. I miss. Of course. When the door opens, I'm lying flat on my face on the floor.

'Miss McCardle, I presume?'

I recognise the voice straight away. It's Mr Feibler, the PE teacher. As I hurry to get up, banging my elbow on a desk so hard I think my arm is going to fall off, all I see is his tanned, hairy legs and his tight, white shorts.

'Yeah, that's me,' I mumble.

'Here's your cellmate. Deborah Lessing.'

'Dobie!' the girl behind him hisses.

Oh no, it's her. Right away, I feel the water from the hose splattering me all over again, my threadbare T-shirt sticking to me, the boys laughing . . . The red haze rises up in front of my eyes. I take a few deep breaths, trying to will it back down again. It's got me into trouble once already at this school. I can't afford to let it take over again. But I remember what Dobie did to me. I can't stand the sight of her. This is going to be the longest detention in history.

I keep my eyes focused on Mr Feibler's snow-white Nikes, because that's safer, and listen as he runs through the rules.

'I hope you've both brought homework to do, or at least a book to read.' A snort from Dobie. 'No talking, no leaving the room. Do either of you want to go to the toilet? Because I've got a basketball team to coach. I can't be running backwards and forwards all afternoon. No? Right. I'll check on you every half hour or so.'

He slams the door behind him and his footsteps speed up. He obviously can't wait to get away from us.

'Every half hour. Yeah, right. We'll be lucky if he comes back at all!'

Well, she would know, wouldn't she? Miss Deborah Lessing, who insists everyone call her Dobie and ignores the ones who call her No-brain. She spends nearly half her afternoons here in this room. I should've remembered that before I went berserk. It's a double punishment, being here with her.

I sit down at the desk in the furthest corner and get out my maths homework. Count this as a blessing, I tell myself, a chance to actually get my homework done properly, in peace. Sometimes it's nearly midnight before I get Mum settled in bed asleep. Homework, by then, gets done in a mad rush.

'You're not actually going to do work, are you?'

She's sitting on the desk by the door, shaking a bottle of dark purple nail polish. I shrug. It's none of her business. 'Don't talk to me.' It snaps out of my mouth before I can stop it.

'Oohh. Afraid I'll corrupt you, sweetie

pie? Too late, you're already in here. In the dungeon with Big Bad Dobie. All hope is gone!' She sneers, making the rings and studs dotted around her face wiggle. When she sticks out her tongue at me, I see the stud through it and my skin crawls.

'Just shut up and leave me alone.' I turn my back on her so I don't have to look at her ugly, studded face. She is such a weirdo, and she plays on it. She likes to put her heavy boots up on her desk to drive the teachers crazy. She's been caught smoking heaps of times.

Everyone said she graffitied the wall behind the teachers' car park with the words 'School sucks, and teachers suck . . .' Half the kids were busting to add their own list of what comes next, but the principal found it in time and got it cleaned off. What Dobie doesn't know is that *I know she didn't do it.* I saw some tenth graders spraying the wall, but she still took the blame. I wondered why, but it served her right. She had to pay for the cleaning, or her parents did. From what I hear, they're revoltingly rich and she gets heaps of pocket money. I hope they made *her* pay for it.

I focus on my algebra, trying to ignore the sharp smell of nail polish. Why am I wasting time thinking about a loser like her? I've got more important things on my mind. Like how I'm going to get home before Mum. Or if I don't, what am I going to tell her? She'll freak out if I tell her I got detention. *Don't call attention to yourself.* She must've said it a million times.

The algebra problem blurs on the page. I blink hard. What time is it? Have I only been here for fifteen minutes? Maybe I'll try English instead. Ms Rogers has been reading *Wuthering Heights* to us in class. She must think most of the kids are too dumb to read it on their own. She's probably right. Now we have to write a poem inspired by the story. I hate this kind of thing. I like to write my poems for myself, not for any stupid teacher to criticise. I close my eyes and force myself to imagine the moors, the wind and the dark trees.

'Hey, you're not writing that for Roger Ramjet's class, are you?' Dobie leans over me and I smell sour cigarettes on her clothes.

'What if I am?' I curl my arm around my notebook.

'You could write one for me. I might even pay you.'

'Get stuffed. Why can't you write your own?'

'Nah, poetry's not my thing. I like songs better.'

'So write a song! Just leave me alone.'

She strolls back to the desk by the door, humming, and dumps her bag down, rummaging through it. I peek over my shoulder, even though I couldn't care less what she's doing. She's flicking through a scruffy notebook, a purple pen in her mouth. She keeps humming the same stupid tune over and over, scribbling every now and then.

She's put me off writing poems now. I'd rather stab her with my pen to get some silence for a change. I go back to algebra, trying to focus on solving the gigantic problem in front of me but it seems like a big mish-mash of letters and numbers that just won't make sense. Once upon a time, I used to be a superstar at maths.

It's her fault I can't concentrate. How am I going to stand being here with her for three whole afternoons? If I'm lucky, this'll be her last day. I ask, 'How long are you in detention for?'

'Huh? Oh, a week this time, I think. I don't know, I lose track.' When she sees my face fall, she says, 'If you can't do the time, don't do the crime.'

'Why are you here so often? Why can't you just...'

'Behave? Conform? Be a little goody like you?'

'I'm not a goody. I . . . I have to . . .'

'Be Mummy's little girl?'

'No! Anyway, what's wrong with getting on OK with your mother?' For me though it's more like mummy-sitting half the time.

She laughs, but it sounds like she's choking. 'Hey, that's why I'm always here. So I don't *have* to go home to my mother.' Her face darkens, she looks away. 'Forget I said that. Go back to your homework, *Goody.*'

Before I can respond, she opens the door and leaves.

I hope Mr Feibler comes back, finds her gone and gives her more detention. It'd serve her right. But somehow I think she wouldn't care at all. Whatever. Not my problem.

My problem might be to get through these three afternoons without killing her.

Scarred Lions
FANIE VILJOEN
A scarred, man-eating lion prowls the game reserve. Will Buyisiwe survive? And heal the wounds from the past?

Stained
JOANNE HICHENS
Crystal is a teenage mum in despair. Can't anyone see the tragedy unfolding? Her only hope is Grace next door.

The Finer Points of Becoming Machine
EMILY ANDREWS
Emma is a mess, like her suicide attempt, but everyone wants her to get better, don't they?

The Only Brother
CAIAS WARD
Sibling rivalry doesn't end at the grave – Andrew is still angry with his only brother, so angry he's hitting out at everyone, including his dad.

The Questions Within
TERESA SCHAEFFER
Scared to be gay?

Thrill Seekers
EDWINA SHAW
Douggie starts hearing voices, and there's nothing Brian can do as he watches his brother and his mates spiral out of control.

Ransom